Hood Love &

Loyalty 3

By: EL Griffin

Messiah

It had been almost 24 hours since that bullshit text from Larissa and there was still no trace of her. My security team was still trying to locate her too. Her phone must have been destroyed or some shit because the tracker wasn't pulling up anything either. That shit was supposed to work whether the phone was on or not.

Even worse it turned out my mama and MJ were connected to Larissa's kidnapping. A couple of niggas came in her house yesterday morning and used them as bait to get at LaLa. Whoever was behind this shit made getting through my damn security look easy as hell.

It seemed like no matter how many mothafuckas I paid, there was always a weakness in my team. Every time they fucked up, my family was put in jeopardy. That shit was eating at me because it was my responsibility to make sure they were safe.

The niggas who came to my mama's house fucked her up pretty bad. She tried to put up a fight and it cost her getting a concussion, a black eye and some bruised ribs. They beat her ass like she was a nigga. That shit made me sick to my stomach to think about. Whoever was involved was gonna get everything back times ten. I put that shit on God. I was thankful MJ was asleep through the entire fucking thing. I didn't even wanna think about what might have happened if he wasn't.

I watched the security tapes from my mama's house over and over again trying to find some damn clue about where the fuck Larissa was and who had her. I really thought I had my family protected. I pulled out all the stops with the security team and even got video surveillance installed in most rooms of all our houses. But all this shit proved that none of it mattered in the end. If one of my enemies wanted to get at me, there was always gonna be a way. I tried not to think about that shit because right now the only thing I needed to focus on was finding my fuckin' wife.

I was still in New York and wasn't leaving until LaLa was found. My little brother was back in NC holding shit down looking after our mama and taking care of MJ until I got back.

The only real lead I had was that Fe's bitch ass was up here. So that nigga needed to be located. Hopefully finding him would lead me to LaLa. I just hoped she was still close and untouched.

I sat on the balcony smoking a blunt and going over messages from my security team when there was a knock at the door. I wasn't expecting anyone so my guard went up. The only shit I planned for the day was to search around the city and a meeting with Jamal for later in the afternoon.

Jamal was the boss up in New York that I added to my team yesterday when we expanded the enterprise. I needed to fill him in on the shit going on with Larissa and get his help. With him and the niggas on his team searching it would only be a matter of time until I got LaLa back.

I put my blunt out and walked over to the door faster than usual. I hoped whoever the fuck was at the door knew something useful. When I looked through the peephole my mood was more fucked up than before if that was even possible. I was ready to kill a mothafucka.

I pulled my Ruger out and held that shit straight out while I opened the fucking door. This dumb mothafucka Antoine really had the nerve to be standing outside my door. He should have known better, especially with how I was feeling right now. His ass was the last nigga alive I wanted to see.

I cocked the hammer back and pointed that shit right between the nigga's eyes. The barrel was only a few inches away from his forehead but the he didn't even fucking blink. He may not be a bitch, but he was stupid as hell for coming to my door thinking shit was cool.

"Pull the fuckin' trigger or put that shit away. I ain't here on no fuck shit bruh, I got something you're gonna wanna hear 'bout Larissa." He said without an ounce of fear in his voice.

"There's no time for the bullshit ya'll on. I need to find my fucking sister." Some nigga standing beside Antoine said.

I hadn't even paid attention to his ass until he spoke up. Usually I stayed on point about my surroundings and took in every detail, but my head was all fucked up right now. I put my weapon down at my side and decided to hear what the fuck they had to say. If the niggas were bold enough to come to my hotel room and face me, maybe whatever they came here for would lead me to getting LaLa back. For Larissa I would put all my damn pride to the side.

I turned towards the one I had never seen to get a better look at his ass. He was light skinned and had the same eyes as Larissa but otherwise they didn't look alike. From the looks of him and his demeanor he was a street nigga like me. But he was dressed in a damn suit like he was into some business or some shit. Larissa never spoke much about her family except saying that her brother and sister moved out as soon as they each turned eighteen. I knew she was on good terms with them and she looked up to them.

8

LaLa's siblings and her grandma were the only family she claimed anymore after all the shit her mother and father put her through. But to me it was fucked up how they left their little sister to deal with everything on her own and just up and left her behind like they did. It wasn't my place to judge if my girl was good then I was good. As long as they didn't do nothing to her to hurt her in the future that is. If that was the case I would handle them both, family or not.

This nigga saying he wanted to find his sister really caught my attention, which is the main reason I decided to hear him out.

I turned around and walked back into the hotel suite towards the living room area. The two of them followed behind me and after I sat down, they each sat in a different chair across from me. The nigga that claimed to be Larissa's brother was the first to speak up. I guess he was serious about not wasting time and I could appreciate that shit. I wasn't trying to waste a moment either especially for these mothafuckas.

"I heard 'bout Larissa being missing and got people looking for her as we speak. I came over here to get all the information you have. Anything, even small could help me find her." He said.

"I don't know you nigga. How do I know you're really who the fuck you say you are.

Talkin' 'bout you got people looking for her. Nigga I got people looking for her. The fuck you take me for?" I said in a calm voice that still held an edge to it.

I wasn't about to sit here and be insulted by this nigga. I wasn't some punk and I would always be respected period. The fact was, I didn't know this man. He may or may not have been telling the truth about who he was. He already had a strike against him for coming here with Antoine's ass even if he was Larissa's brother. I didn't know who he really was or how the fuck he knew about LaLa being gone. He needed to clear up some shit before I believed his ass and told him a damn thing.

I guess he got the message that I wasn't about to budge and wasn't gonna give his ass any information. Apparently he came prepared for me not believing who he was. He pulled out two pictures from his jacket pocket and held them out for me to take.

I looked both of the pictures over without commenting on either. One of the pictures was of three little kids and the girl in the middle standing between the two other children favored Larissa. But the kids were all too young to really tell if it was her for sure. The other picture was more recent and I knew for a fact that the girl in the picture was Larissa. She looked to be about thirteen or something. When most kids that age were going through an awkward stage and looked funny as hell, my baby already looked like she was on her way to becoming the beautiful woman she was now.

The nigga sitting across from me was legit. He was LaLa's brother. So I would hear him out. But him coming here with Antoine's ass still wasn't sitting right with me. After he explained that shit, I would decide if I was gonna tell his ass anything. I didn't trust many mothafuckas and wasn't about to tell him some shit that would end up putting Larissa in more danger, no matter if he was her brother or not. I handed the pictures back over to him.

"I'm Larissa's brother Enzo." He said after he put the pictures away and looked back in my direction. "Look, I don't know you and you don't know me. But I'm gonna find my damn sister you can bet on that shit. I'm just trying to get all the information I can to bring her home safe." He continued.

"I'm guessing you already know who I am. But you fucked up bringing this nigga with you. So before I say shit, I'm gonna need for you to clear some shit up for me. How the fuck you know this nigga?" I asked referring to Antoine.

I wasn't saying a damn thing until I heard some shit that made sense. I was gonna find Larissa without her brother's help anyway. I would still tell him what was up since it was only right and he was her brother. But only if there was a good reason why he was here with a nigga that I considered an enemy. If I didn't like his answer then it was "fuck him" too, whether he was LaLa's brother or not.

"Me and Antoine go way back. To keep shit real I'm not some regular ass street nigga. Larissa don't even know this shit... we're part of the Colombo family on our mother's side. Not just a small part either. Our grandfather is head of the family. I'm in the business now and have the full backing of our family. As far as Antoine, I'm his supplier. He's here because I know him and my sister used to be involved with each other. So when I heard about the shit with Larissa, I came to him trying to find out what the fuck happened. He brought me here because he said they wasn't together anymore and that she was with your ass." Enzo told me.

He was the Italian connection backing Antoine that I heard about when that nigga's name first came up back home. Everything he said checked out but it didn't mean I liked the shit I was hearing. It was fucked up that Larissa's brother knew about what Antoine and Larissa used to have going on and they weren't even really together like we were. It rubbed me the wrong way for some reason that he knew about them, but not about me and her being together. I always made it my fucking mission to let every mothafucka know who my woman was. I decided to push my feelings to the side and tell him the information I knew.

If the shit he told me about their family was all true then that meant he might be able to help find LaLa sooner. I was willing to get past my pride for LaLa's benefit at least for right now. I was still planning on killing Antoine's ass, but it could wait until after she was back home safe.

I went ahead and told Enzo everything I knew from the last message she sent to not being able to pull up the tracker on her phone. He said he was gonna get on the shit right away and keep me posted if anything came up. With the Italians and all my team including the new boss, Jamal's team, on the lookout it was really only a matter of time before she was back home where she belonged.

After I finished telling Enzo all the shit I knew, him and Antoine stood to leave. I got up and shook LaLa's brother's hand before he left. Antoine began walking back towards the door behind him. I ignored him being in my damn presence while I was discussing shit with LaLa's brother. But I was a real nigga and wasn't about to play pussy no matter what the fuck was going on. I was already acting out of character letting mothafuckas step to me like this. Before he even took two steps, I went ahead and stepped in front of him blocking his path. He stopped in his tracks just like I fucking wanted.

"When this shit said and done, ain't no saving you nigga." I said to his ass referring to my intention of killing him.

I didn't wanna go back and forth with this nigga ever again in my lifetime. I'm sure he knew what the fuck I really meant by that shit. He knew what was up and how I got down from my reputation. This mothafucka continued to disrespect me time and time again. Even him coming here, was disrespectful in my opinion. No matter what the reason was for him being here, the fact was he should never show his face around me if he wanted to keep breathing.

"Whatever nigga. Brother or not, I'm not some bitch ass nigga that's gonna answer to your ass. Get the fuck out my way." He responded back as he stepped around me.

Normally that would have been lights out for his ass on the spot, but I let that shit slide again. He kept getting spared but eventually I would catch up to his ass. I never made empty threats. What I spoke was the mothafuckin' truth. I was somewhat caught off guard with him talking that shit about being my brother. He must have figured that shit out somehow. But I was glad he didn't think that shit changed a damn thing between us. I still felt like he violated me with coming to NC in the first place. Then he had to be the only other nigga who ever fucked with my ol' lady.

After the two of them left, I headed out right behind them. I needed to get up with Jamal and give him all the information I had about Larissa being taken, even if it wasn't much. He had five teams around the city alone that answered to him. Since we were now doing business together and part of the same organization his teams were now also under me technically. So it made sense for me to use my clout to help find LaLa and whoever the fuck was behind the shit.

Carina

I stood over the bed smiling down at the bitch that made my life a living hell over the past year. I was finally getting back at her for all the bad shit she caused to happen. Money's bitch, Larissa laid completely still while her arms and legs were tied to the headboard and foot of the bed. She was completely naked since we stripped that bitch down after we dragged her ass down here yesterday.

Looking at her light skin that was now covered with bruises from the kicks and punches I landed yesterday was turning me on. She was sexy as hell and I liked the fact that she was hurting behind the shit I was doing to her even more. I was never into bitches before, but seeing her tied up and spread wide being held against her will gave me a rush. It was like a drug, the shit was the best feeling in the world to me.

I knew her hoe ass was pregnant too. I could see her small baby bump and noticed how she held her stomach when I was beating her ass in the van. I didn't give a fuck about that damn bastard she was carrying either. She took my man, then ended up getting Torio killed and he was the only man who really ever understood me to begin with. Before I killed her ass I was gonna make her wish she never met Money's ass. Fuck her and that baby.

I leaned down and slapped the shit out of one of her exposed thighs to get her to wake up. Her eyes immediately shot open. Once she focused on me her stare turned cold. I had to give it to the bitch she didn't cower away like I would have thought. Shit I would have been begging trying to do anything to get myself out of the same situation if it was me. She should have realized that no matter what kinda look she gave me, I didn't give a fuck about her suffering. It wasn't gonna do shit to change her fate. I pulled the knife from my back pocket and held it down close to her stomach.

"Should I kill your baby now or have some fun first?" I asked her.

Since the bitch's mouth was gagged she couldn't answer and all I heard was a mumbling. She was shaking her head back and forth in an attempt to say no. I grinned down at her and then moved my free hand down to her pussy.

I stuck three of my fingers all the way in penetrating her walls, while I still held the knife close to her stomach. I didn't care that the shit was hurting her. I wanted her to feel violated and hurt, the way she hurt me by taking away everything I loved. I continued to work my hand in and out of her while looking at the cold stare that she was sending my way.

The bitch started getting wet as fuck too making my pussy throb. So I started going harder and faster. The fear that I knew I was causing only fueled the shit I was doing to her even more.

I set the knife down on top of her stomach and let my other hand unzip my own jeans. I slipped my fingers between my pussy folds and began rubbing on my own clit to match the shit I was doing to her. I continued to watch the expressions on her face. I saw nothing but pain, but her body was responding to me. The nasty bitch was loving what I was doing to her on some level. I kept moving my hands and was on the verge of cumming myself when the basement door swung open.

Fe's ass came in and I heard him get close to the bed where I was fucking with Money's bitch. I reluctantly pulled my hand out of my pants and out of the stupid hoe's pussy too. I looked back over my shoulder in his direction.

"Don't stop on my account. I love a good show." Fe said in his deep accent.

"I got more shit planned for the bitch don't worry. But playtime's over." I replied back to his ass before I moved forward on the bed and gripped that bitch by the throat.

I squeezed my hand tight as hell making sure to cut off her air supply. I held my grip and whispered in her ear, "You're a nasty bitch, you liked that shit. Wait 'til next time. I won't be so easy on your ass."

I took the gag out of her mouth and kissed her hard as hell sticking my tongue as deep as it would go down her throat. I wanted her to feel abused and helpless. I had never done no shit like this in my life, but I was loving the power I had over her. I had her life in the palm of my hands and could do whatever the fuck I wanted to her and she couldn't do shit about it. For the first time I felt truly free.

The stupid bitch decided to be brave and bit down on my tongue as it was in her mouth causing it to bleed. I flipped the fuck out when I saw the blood pouring from my mouth and I started punching her over and over in the face. I reached for the knife and was planning on slitting the bitch's damn throat.

"No, No. We need the girl." Fe said while pulling me off the hoe.

I was breathing heavy as hell from putting in that work and beating the bitch's ass before he pulled me off. Finally my breathing calmed, while I stood there looking down at Money's bitch.

Fe was right we needed to keep her alive a little while longer so that we could get the money we were gonna ransom her for. Don't ask me why, but Money was weak behind this bitch. We were gonna make him think that he was gonna get her back, but once we had our hands on the cash the bitch was dead. I was gonna be the one to make that shit happen too.

I stepped over to bed again and looked down one last time before turning around and walking away with Fe behind me. Once we were outside the basement door he turned and locked the door leaving her tied up and passed out from the pain I had just inflicted on her.

Larissa

When I woke up and came face to face with Messiah's ex I was in so much pain. But more than the pain, I felt a deep seeded anger. I wanted to kill this bitch staring down at me more than I ever thought I would want to hurt someone. She shot me when I was pregnant before and now here I was pregnant again and in danger all over again. The irony of the situation wasn't sitting well with me. I wasn't the type of woman who sat back taking shit anymore. The old Larissa was gone. I was tied up now, but when I had my chance I was killing everyone who was responsible.

My entire body was hurting especially my face. I could tell I had a black eye since it was puffy and almost completely closed up. I pulled at my arms and feet and felt the tight ropes dig into my skin.

I was completely naked since those two sick ass people tore my clothes from my body while I was laying on the dirty basement floor. They did all that after they dragged me down the flight of stairs to the basement below. I tried to put up a fight but it was two against one and no matter how much I struggled against them, I couldn't get the upper hand.

Carina was really evil. She was capable of even more than I ever thought possible. Me and Messiah both had underestimated her. I couldn't help but think back to the night I thought I saw her out at the club. I should have searched for her ass and tracked her down like Shanice wanted to do. I was way too confident in myself since I had gotten a gun of my own. But now I was paying for that mistake and I knew exactly how sick she was.

She held that knife to my stomach with a look of eagerness in her eyes. She really was gonna kill my ass, but she wanted to make me suffer as much as possible. I didn't know what I had ever done that was so bad to her that she wanted to put me through all this shit. But it didn't' matter. Her intentions were clear.

Then she violated me by touching me and making my body respond knowing I was helpless. The sick thing was she liked that shit too. At this point I was scared beyond belief about what would happen to me next. Laying here and thinking about what her or that man were gonna do to me was making me lose my mind.

In order for me to survive and get out of this situation I needed to push all my feelings for myself to the back of my mind and become numb. I would not let them see the fear I felt no matter what they did to me, I silently vowed to myself.

I needed to do whatever I could to last long enough for Messiah to find me. I didn't doubt his ability to get to me. I just hoped he made it in time. I heard Carina talk about keeping me alive. So for right now they needed me. I said another silent prayer asking God to protect me and my unborn before drifting off to sleep again not knowing what I would wake up to next.

Messiah

I was out scouring the streets with Jamal. Silk and Draco's ass were searching and asking around too trying to come up with something. Even though our operations had merged and were now both under Money Maker's Inc. New York still wasn't the same as being home. I could ask questions, look around, but shit I didn't hold the power and respect that Jamal did up here. That was why I needed him with me to put fear into these nigga's hearts out here so we could get some kind of fuckin' lead on where Larissa was.

I was smoking a blunt and pulling up all the information my security team had sent in the last hour. The only thing they found was a van that had LaLa's purse in it with her phone smashed inside. They sent me pictures of the shit and when I saw her bloody clothes laying on the floor of the van I almost lost my fuckin' mind. It was obvious that the mothafuckas wanted me to find this shit. The only thing I could hope is that they wanted to make some kind of deal or wanted some damn money or something.

I still thought that it was Fe behind this shit, but really it could be anyone. I knew that Fe was up in New York and I was already planning on taking his ass out after the meeting the other day. But the security I had on him lost him right before the sit down. He somehow eluded my whole fuckin' team and that shit made it seem more and more likely that he was the one who took Larissa.

Plus the nigga who did this shit had to have enough power and reach to send some people to my mama's house. Fe was on the outs with my pops and the cartel in Belize, but he still had some loyal followers and family in New York.

That's where I was headed now. Jamal knew where his people stayed. I guess they were related to his ass through marriage or some shit. None of that shit mattered to me one bit. I would kill every last one of them if it meant bringing LaLa back safe.

When we turned onto the street leading to Mott Haven in South Bronx, Jamal let me know this was where Fe's relations lived. I was more than ready to make shit happen and get some answers. I didn't know who in his family stayed here, but if there was a chance they could help me get LaLa back I was willing to do whatever it took. Even if I was out of my element in a whole other fuckin' state.

If Fe really was behind this shit, he should have known better than coming against me a second time. I was far from the same up and coming boss I was before that shit in Miami. Now I was sitting on a damn throne compared to that shit.

Once the car came to a stop, me and Jamal hopped out the ride. Two of his niggas that were riding in the backseat followed behind us. Jamal reassured me over and over that we didn't' have shit to worry about anywhere we went in the city since he ran all the shit. But I was always cautious. Our business dealings were still new, and in the game you couldn't trust any mothafucka further than you could see them.

I was carrying my heat in the back of my pants like usual and a compact nine up in my dreads. I used having dreads to my advantage and would put them up and hide my heat in them whenever I felt the need. I didn't know none of these niggas that well. For all I knew, they could be setting my ass up and I wasn't trying to get caught slipping again.

We walked down the path leading to the entrance to the building. As we walked past the people outside it was evident that Jamal wasn't bullshittin' when he said we didn't have to worry about nothing. Everybody spoke and greeted him with respect.

I watched the way he interacted with them too and was impressed with how he carried himself. He was a confident boss but he wasn't looking down on anybody that approached him. Even the heads that tried to get money from his ass that a lot of nigga look down on, he still showed respect. That was exactly the type of nigga I wanted on my team. You could be a boss and not act like you were better than anyone. It was important that a person not forget where they come from no matter how good or bad they're doing in life.

Jamal stopped in front of a door on the second floor and looked over at me.

"This where they at. I got word there's two women and some kids in here now. However you wanna handle this shit, I got you." He let me know.

We already discussed what I was gonna do but you never knew what was gonna happen. You could plan all day long, but shit always could go left. I didn't plan on touching the kids and didn't really wanna fuck with the bitches either. Hurting and killing women and children wasn't really my thing. But when it was all said and done I was willing to do whatever the fuck it took to get Larissa back no matter what it was. Fe fucked up when he came after my family.

I knocked on the door and waited for some kind of answer. Not one sound came from inside the apartment. I knocked a few more times before my patience ran out. I pulled out my pistol. My shit already had the silencer attached so I shot right at the door handle causing that shit to instantly bust open.

If Jamal's information was solid then there was women and kids in the apartment. They had to be hiding for a reason. If they didn't have any reason to hide they would have just come to the door, so my instincts were telling me Fe was behind the shit without a doubt.

I stepped into the living room area and saw two women sitting there all calm and composed like the fact that their door being shot open wasn't shit. They didn't look up from the TV show that was on or anything. I stepped around in front of them both and finally the younger one sitting on the couch looked up. I had to admit she was bad as fuck too. She had a sexy dark complexion and even though she was sitting down I could see all that ass she had on her. She was thicker than LaLa but I liked a bitch who had some meat on her. I wasn't here to fuck though and no matter how the bitch looked she wasn't shit to me. But the fact that there was this young beautiful girl here made me wonder who she was to Fe.

I asked her straight out, "Where's Fe?"

Instead of answering me the bitch stood up and spit in my face from only inches away. I wiped that shit off and then used my hand holding my heat to back hand her with the barrel knocking her back down onto the couch. As soon as that shit went down the two niggas Jamal brought with him pulled their heat out and trained their guns on the women.

I walked away from where the women were in the living room and started searching around the apartment looking for the two kids that were supposed to be there. I bet they were hiding somewhere, which was the same thing I would have my kids doing if it was me in the same situation. I went into one of the bedrooms and looked in the closet and under the bed but no one was in there. I made my way across the hall to another room and when I opened the closet I found the kids. I really wasn't trying to hurt them so I hoped their mother cooperated with the shit I was asking. If she did then no harm would come to them.

I picked them up without a problem even though both their asses were kicking and screaming. They had to be around three years old and must have been twins since they looked alike. They were about the same size but one was a girl and the other a boy.

When I came back out into the living room I set both of the kids down and they went running to their mother. She started crying and hugging both of them. Finally, she looked back up at me standing in front of her and told her kids to go to their grandma in Garifuna.

I was standing there quietly taking everything in. I didn't want shit to go bad so hopefully realizing her kids were now in play would be enough to get the bitch talking.

"I don't know where he is. What do you want from me?" The woman asked me.

"Call his ass. Get him on the line, then give me the phone." I told her ass.

She pulled out her cell phone and put it to her ear after placing the call. As soon as she said hello into the phone I snatched that shit from her. I needed to let the mothafucka know what was at stake. I already put shit together, and figured that this bitch was either his daughter or niece or some shit. So that made the kids his grandchildren. I could cut out his whole fuckin' line if I wanted. So if he had Larissa he better fuckin' make sure she was good and made it back home unharmed.

"Where the fuck's my wife nigga?" I got straight to the point.

"It's good to hear from you Money. I was getting ready to call you. I have a proposition for you." Fe replied. Making it clear that he did have LaLa.

"Fuck you and your proposition. I got your fuckin' family. So you gonna do exactly what they fuck I tell yo' ass. I want Larissa brought back to the hotel and she better be untouched nigga." I don't know why he thought he still had the upper hand when he knew his relation just called from her phone.

"I don't give a fuck about that whore or those little bastards. I want fifty million boy. Then I'll consider letting her go after I have my fun with her. Leave the money where the van was found in a black duffle bag at 9:00 tomorrow morning." He said after laughing and then hung up.

The shit he said only made me more pissed off. To send a message I turned and shot that bitch in the head as soon as the call ended. I needed to be heartless to get it through his head I wasn't fucking around. The kids started screaming and crying. They ran over to their mother and tried to wake her up. I used her phone to take a picture and sent a message to Fe's ass with the shit clear as day. He might have played like it was all good, but he could have been putting on an act. I wasn't gonna do shit to the kids but he didn't know that.

With the message I let him know I was keeping the kids until I got LaLa back and I would drop the money in the morning like he instructed. I wasn't trying to play with LaLa's life. That amount of money wasn't shit to me. I expected her to be back at the hotel before the drop was even complete and I sent that nigga those instruction too. That way he would make sure she made it back to me safe.

Jamal's team went ahead and took the kids and the old lady out of the apartment and put them in another ride behind the one we rode over in. After they were secured I parted ways with Jamal and his niggas.

I wanted to get back to the hotel and call back home to make sure MJ was still good. I was thankful to have my little bro step up and take care of both him and my mama while I got LaLa back. He reassured me that MJ was good and things were looking up as far as my mother's condition too. She was awake and feeling better.

Once I hung up the phone I went ahead and pulled up my laptop. I needed to transfer the fifty mill to my checking account so that I could withdraw that shit first thing in the morning when the bank opened. It was gonna be cutting it close since they didn't open until 8:30 and Fe's bitch ass set the drop for 9. Every time I let myself think about the shit he said my head ended up in a dark place thinking about the shit he said was fuckin' with me. I didn't want to think about him doing shit to Larissa.

Shanice

My mind was on overdrive thinking about Larissa. I couldn't help but fear the worst for her and it felt like I was losing my damn sister again. This shit was the second time her life was in danger in only a year. Everything had been going so good for the most part too, until that bitch came to the dinner the other night.

Money came by our hotel room a little while ago and told both me and Silk all about the shit Fe said earlier. Even though that nigga said he was gonna let Larissa go tomorrow morning, I didn't trust nothing he said. I was hoping and praying that everything went smooth and he would stay true to the shit he said. But I wasn't counting on it.

The fact that Money was willing to give so much money away in order to try and bring my best friend home didn't surprise me either. He loved her enough to give away his last dime and all that he had. The kind of love they shared is what I was hoping to have with my man.

I was lying in bed completely naked waiting for Silk to get out the shower. It had become a habit to sleep naked, it was just more comfortable to me. I was sitting up enough to where I wouldn't spill the glass of wine I was drinking. Wine had become my escape since going through the breakup with Silk and even now it helped me cope when shit was going on. I didn't have a drinking problem or anything but whenever I was stressed, a glass or two would let my mind rest and calm my nerves. I was scrolling through my phone and consumed with nothing in particular when Silk made his way over to the bed and laid down next to me straight out the shower.

"It's gonna be alright ma. Money got shit under control and Larissa will be back home safe tomorrow. You ain't gotta stress the shit."

He said that shit trying to comfort me. Then he began rubbing on my thighs and massaging the muscles in them making my entire body relax under his touch.

"I hope you're right." I commented back.

Even though Silk was trying to reassure me that everything was gonna work out, it didn't feel that way. Last time Larissa was shot she went through being in a fucking coma and shit. Now here she was being kidnapped and it was unlikely that she was gonna be unharmed completely. I knew all about how the street life was dangerous, but damn it was like she couldn't catch a break for nothing.

This was the life she chose to be a part of but it was times like this that made me question her decision and mine for that matter as far as being with niggas that were like ours. But there was no way either of us was walking away even if it cost us our lives. I knew that shit too. I really just wanted her back safe and sound with her family.

I needed to get my mind off of the situation so I leaned over and started kissing Silk slow and deep. Letting the feelings he caused from rubbing my thighs to take over my thoughts. He got the message and moved both of his hands over my body caressing my breasts.

He cupped each one and paid them attention sucking and kissing on them rough. Shit he was even biting down on them making my body squirm to get away. I wanted to savor in this moment as long as possible and escape from the shit going on around us.

Silk moved his hands down to my pussy and started kissing his way down. He made his way from my stomach down below my waistline and I opened my eyes back up to watch. I placed my hands on top of his head and started running my hands over his deep waves. Then my sexy nigga really started going to work eating the fuck out of my pussy.

I wrapped my legs around his back automatically since what he was doing to me was so intense. He latched onto my clit and that shit really drove me wild. I was on the verge of cumming and then he stuck two fingers in my pussy sending me over the edge. Once my cum was gushing out he let up and waited until I was done before diving back in and licking all around trying to catch it all.

Since I was already naked I wanted him to be too. I was gonna return the favor, so I pushed him back aggressively and then lifted his Tee over his head. While my breasts was in his face he started playing with them again before I made my way lower and slid the boxers off his legs. He went to help me out but I swatted his hand away. I was gonna take care of my man. I got up off the bed and reached out for him to take my hand and stand too.

He got up and towered over me. I dropped down and stayed squatting. I began stroking his dick with one hand and playing with his balls with the other. That only made his dick get harder if that was possible so I opened wide and let that shit hit the back of my throat.

His dick always made me choke a little but that shit made me go harder. I swirled my tongue and flicked it around while I worked my jaws and picked up the pace. Spit was dripping down so I worked my hand while moving up and down letting it get nasty. I continued to alternate between sucking and licking moving faster and faster. His dick started jumping so I knew he was close. I wanted to catch every drop so I suctioned my mouth even more before his cum shot out and I swallowed it all down.

Silk leaned forward and gripped me by the arms rough as hell getting me to stand up. He backed me up into our dresser and turned me around. I looked ahead into the mirror above the dresser and our eyes met right before he stuck his dick balls deep in my pussy.

The shit was so big it forced me to scream out and my walls clamped down until I adjusted. I leaned forward onto the dresser for support while he slow stroked me nice and deep. With both of his hands he gripped my ass cheeks spreading me wider and lifting me up some. He had my ass tooted up and me on my damn toes not able to move besides taking the dick.

"Look at this shit Shanice." He demanded.

So I looked back up into the mirror and got even more turned on. My breasts were bouncing with each stroke he gave and the shit made me throw my ass back as much as possible. Even though he was hurting me I loved it. I bent all the way forward and leaned down against the dresser letting my stomach and breasts rest on it completely. Arching my back as much as I could with the limited space I began letting my pussy pop for my nigga while he fucked me. I loved this man's dick.

He slapped me hard on the ass and then grabbed ahold of my hips. Silk pulled me back into him giving me another few deep ass strokes before he released inside me. He stayed planted inside me for a minute before sliding his dick out. I still felt like I couldn't move when he backed away and he knew that shit too.

"It ain't that bad girl, stop being a baby and get your ass over here. I'll make your feel better." Silk said trying to be funny.

Wasn't shit funny though. He really fucked me up when he fucked me good and knew my legs were always weak afterwards. It was always like that whenever we fucked standing up. I stayed right where the fuck I was and turned around enough to flip his ass off. He immediately came back over and scooped my ass up like it was nothing and threw me over his damn shoulder like it was nothing. His arrogant ass threw me down onto the bed after that. I couldn't do nothing but laugh at his silly ass.

"Is that better baby?" He said emphasizing the word baby.

I really loved Silk's ass. We could fuck then joke around and just always had a good vibe going on. After shaking my head yes I got back comfortable on the bed. Silk came out of the bathroom with a rag to clean me off with. He always treated me like a queen and loved to cater to me, just like I did him. Once settled back in I reached over for my phone on the bedside table. Silk was going through his phone and flipped the TV on to Sports Center.

I saw that I had one unread message. When I opened the shit up I was more than surprised. My ex Deandre had reached out with a simple text but it was enough to fuck up my mood, even after getting dicked down properly.

It read, "Hit me up, we need to talk. Love u girl."

I didn't know what kind of bullshit that nigga was on, but he could forget whatever we once had. I moved on and was happy. I was happier than I had ever been.

When me and Dre were together things were all good in the beginning. He was my first everything. Anything he needed me to do, I did no questions asked. I was his rider and held him down even when he was locked up for a year. It turned out everything I thought we had was a lie. His ass was cheating on me and even had a baby on me. Once I found that shit out I bounced. When I said I never was a fool for a nigga that was the truth. I didn't do that dumb in love shit. So whatever he wanted to talk about wasn't gonna happen.

I didn't hold no hate towards him, but I definitely didn't want nothing to do with his ass. He dogged me out in the worst way and now I knew what it was really like to be loved and treated right. There was no way I would be going backward. I decided not to tell Silk about it because there was nothing for him to worry about. I didn't plan on communicating back with Deandre's ass.

I deleted the message and blocked the number he sent it from. The last thing I needed was Dre trying to come back in the picture and fuck things up for me. Especially when me and Silk just got back on good terms. We still had work to do to get back the trust a hundred percent and I wasn't gonna chance that.

On top of that, right now we needed to focus on finding my best friend and making sure she came back safe and sound. I knew Silk was worried about her too. Larissa had become like a sister to him too. We were all like one big family. With the street lifestyle we were deep into, you had to be like family. We all depended on each other to protect each other. Our niggas were the real fucking deal so we were all we had.

Thinking about Larissa again got me all the way back in the funk I was in before. I wanted morning to hurry up and get here.

Larissa

Something was off. I had been lying awake in the same bed my kidnappers tied me to for what seemed like a few hours and my stomach just wasn't feeling right. Lately I was feeling little flutters of my baby moving but now it was like nothing. I couldn't reach down and rub my stomach or move much at all since my hands and feet were tied to the posts of the bed. I prayed over and over begging God to protect my unborn and that nothing was wrong with him or her.

Tears started flowing from my eyes again and I couldn't even wipe them away. I was in such a fucked up situation. After a few minutes of feeling sorry for myself I got myself together again and reminded myself that I had to be strong to get through this. I needed to get back to Messiah and MJ. The thought of those two were keeping me motivated.

The basement door swung open and I turned my head as much as I could to see whether it was that evil bitch Carina or who I assumed was Fe. This time it was Fe walking over towards me. He didn't look like the same calm and composed man from earlier when he stopped Carina from hurting me more than she already had. He looked stressed out and on edge, but also angry.

Once he was near the bed where I was strapped to he stopped and took off his suit jacket and rolled up his shirt sleeves to what looked like a very expensive suit. He ran one of his hands through his greying hair.

"So your boyfriend wants you back unharmed. But since he struck first, it's only right he feels pain for what he's done, don't you think?" He asked more as a command than an actual question.

It was hard to understand him but I was getting the point he was trying to make. He planned on doing some shit to me to make Messiah pay. My mouth was free of the gag since Carina's nasty ass kissed me earlier so I chose to try and talk some sense into him. I didn't know what he was capable of, but I had a feeling he would try and really hurt me to get at Messiah.

"Please, I'm pregnant. Just let me go. I'll get you whatever you want. Any amount of money!" I begged.

"It's too late. Money will get you back, but he must pay." He responded.

Fe then took off his shoes and pulled down his pants. I knew what his undressing meant. He was about to rape me. I had already been violated by Carina and now I was really gonna get raped by this man and I was in a position that I couldn't even fight back. I was completely helpless.

"No! No! Please." I pleaded again.

All Fe did was position himself on top of me and cover my mouth with one of his hands. He then penetrated me like the shit wasn't nothing to him. It didn't matter that I was begging or crying, the sick ass mothafucka didn't give a fuck about any of that. All he wanted was to make Messiah pay by violating me. He started pumping in and out of me while I was struggling to breathe with his hand still covering my mouth and part of my nose.

I turned my head to the side and that's when I saw Carina standing near the foot of the bed with a phone in her hand. That evil bitch was recording me being raped. I couldn't think about what was happening to me, so instead I closed my eyes and tried to think about my son while Fe had his way with me.

The sick bastard started enjoying the shit too. He began kissing on my neck and rubbing my breasts. I was so repulsed by what he was doing that my pussy was dry and the shit was hurting even worse. His dick wasn't even that big but it felt like I was being torn in half. When his body tensed up he finally pulled out of me and jacked himself off until his cum shot out all over my face and stomach.

I opened my eyes and looked Carina right in the eyes. She didn't have one look of remorse that any sane woman would have for another woman being raped. Instead she started laughing.

"Money's ass won't want you now. Your hoe ass liked that shit too." She said.

Fe got back dressed and left like nothing even happened. I wished Carina would leave to, but of course shit was not going the way I wanted at all. Instead she set the phone down and came over to where I was laying. She reached over in the corner where it looked like some dirty old tools were kept. Then she sat down towards the foot of the bed and held the hammer she grabbed by the top part. At this point I didn't even care what she did to me. I was numb to everything going on. My body and spirit had been broken. I had never been so abused and ashamed in my life.

She stood over me and pulled the hammer she brought from the table back and then swung it down as hard as she could against my stomach. She brought it down over and over again while I screamed for her to stop. I was in so much pain and then I felt the blood leaking out between my legs and knew immediately I was losing the baby.

She still didn't stop. My whole body cramped up and I started screaming out in the worst pain I ever felt. It felt like I was dying. I guess my screams were loud enough that Fe heard them because he came running in. I heard him shouting at Carina before I lost consciousness and the pain went away.

Messiah (Money)

After everything was said and done I was gonna make anyone involved with taking Larissa pay. Having my security team and Jamal's crews on the lookout for information paid off. It was five o'clock in the morning and Me, Silk and Draco were on our way to a house over near the projects I was at yesterday. It turned out Fe and Carina were a lot fucking closer than I thought. They were stupid enough to come after my heart and not even try and hide out for real.

They mistook me for some punk ass nigga that didn't have the power I really did. Their misjudgments were their second mistake. I planned on getting Larissa out of harm's way and keeping both their asses alive long enough to really torture them for this shit.

We rented out a big ass Suburban for the purpose of transporting the mothafuckas all the way back to NC. I would have a couple trustworthy niggas on my team make the eight hour drive. Driving straight through until they reached the town outside our warehouse where I would take over driving the rest of the way. A simple death was too easy for both Carina and Fe. They better hope that LaLa wasn't hurt in any way either or the shit would be ten times worse.

Draco reached up front to hand me the blunt. When it was all said and done he still was one of my day ones and that was why he was gonna continue to be on my team. He did some questionable shit when it came to bringing that bitch Che to dinner, but over the course of the last couple days he stepped up. He was like my brother out here and had been helping try and find Larissa which made it easier to look past his fuck up. I wasn't trusting him a hundred percent, for the time being his ass was still on thin ice. I believed everybody's true colors came through in time.

I grabbed ahold of the blunt and only took a couple pulls before passing it over to Silk who was sitting beside me like usual. I needed to calm my nerves a little in case some shit was foul when I found Larissa. I didn't want to think any negative shit though so I chose to focus back on the task at hand.

"Draco, I want you and Silk to approach the front of the house and knock on the door like shit's good. We don't know who's all in there. Play the shit off like you some friends of Fe if it turns out there's more mothafuckas in there then just them two. If either Fe or Carina open the door find a way to make shit happen fast. I'm gonna go around the back and find a way in."

All the intel we had said that Fe and Carina were the only two seen going in and out of the spot we were heading over to. But there could have been more people inside. We really were going into this shit blind. But just like when we went and got MJ from Torio's bitch ass I wasn't gonna sit back and waste time thinking about the shit.

The fact was those mothafuckas had Larissa and whether I came out of the shit alive or not didn't fuckin' matter as long as she was good. I was appreciative to have my niggas with me, and knew they felt the exact same way about the shit. We were all a damn family out here and they looked at LaLa like a little sister themselves.

Since it was early as hell there wasn't many people out yet which worked in our favor too. The sun wasn't even up yet. The only people out were the heads and the hustlas that worked for Jamal, so no word was gonna get to Fe before we made our move.

After pulling up a house over from the place Larissa was allegedly in, I parked the car just across the street. All three of us pulled out our heat and exited the vehicle. It was time to get my fuckin' wife back and take care of these two that had been a damn thorn in my side for the last year.

Draco and Silk approached the front of the house and walked up to the door without making a damn sound. I walked around the side of the house with my gun drawn and heard them knocking. I bet whoever was inside was asleep. That would be to our advantage too. I started looking inside the windows that didn't have curtains and saw a basement window near the back of the house. When I leaned over and wiped the dirt and grit off the window I couldn't really see shit. That was gonna be the first place I looked for LaLa once I was inside.

When I got to the backside there was a small little step up to the back door. I couldn't hear nothing going on in the front of the house back there so I tried my luck and turned the door knob. It was locked but it was a basic handle nothing hard to break into. I pulled out one of my credit cards and slid that shit up just like I used to do when I was a kid and locked out of my house and it opened up with no problem.

I stepped inside the dark ass room. The shit was pitch black except for the little bit of moonlight still shining coming through the door I just entered in through. From what I could make out, I was standing inside the kitchen. There was another door just to the side of where I was standing and I hoped it was the one that led to the basement. I still didn't hear shit coming from any other part of the house. So I stayed as quiet as possible while I pulled the door open.

The steps led down and I kept my gun drawn as I walked down the old rickety ass steps. Each step I took created a squeaking noise but I needed to see what was down here. When I got to the bottom of the steps it turned out the basement was finished off and there was two different doors on either side of where I was standing. I turned the one to my left that had to be closer to where the window I looked through was at. It was unlocked and I walked through moving faster than I had been before.

Inside it was even darker than upstairs. It was clear that there wasn't anybody else in the basement, otherwise my ass would have been blasted already. With my free hand I pulled my cell phone out to use the flashlight on it and saw a bed over in the corner. There was rope tied to the head and foot of the bed. As I walked closer to the shit I saw that the mattress was soaked through with blood and laying near the top part there was the bracelet LaLa always wore that had both our initials on it.

The sight of the bed and her jewelry drove me over the edge. I snatched up the bracelet and put it in my pocket before turning back around and storming up the steps that led back upstairs. I didn't give a fuck if anyone heard me at this point. It was obvious some horrible shit happened to Larissa and I was ready to murder all the mothafuckas involved in the shit. I still needed to find where the fuck she was at too. I said a quick silent prayer that she was still alive because the amount of blood I saw wasn't good.

When I reached the top of the stairs I heard Draco and Silk talking shit to some bitch over towards the front of the house. I made my way closer to where their voices were coming from and was able to see Carina's ass on her knees in front of Draco. He had his pistol pulled and pointed against the bitch's forehead. Silk was asking her where Larissa and Fe were. There wasn't time for the bitch to stall. We needed to find Larissa now.

"Where the fuck's my wife bitch?" I shouted as I came up behind Carina.

I grabbed her by her weave and yanked that shit back as hard as I could. She looked up into my eyes. When I came into her view, I saw the recognition and fear that crossed her face.

"Fuck you and that bitch!" She had the nerve to say.

"Where the fuck is she? That's the last time I'm gonna ask. I got niggas posted at your house right now Carina. You either tell me what I wanna know or it's lights out for your sister and Monae." I told her ass.

She knew I was serious too. Monae wasn't my child and even though I used to feel a bond with her, that was gone when it came

51

to my family. I didn't like the thought of having a baby's death on my hands. But at the end of the day I was willing to do whatever it took to get LaLa back no matter what. My conscious would just have to deal with whatever that ended up being.

"You wouldn't do that. You love Monae." She stammered out while I just stood looking down at her with a raised eyebrow.

I pulled my phone back out and held it out ready to call the niggas on my team to make that shit happen.

"Fine nigga! She's at the hospital. She's a nasty bitch too, Money. You gotta see the shit on my phone." Carina confessed with an evil ass smile on her face."

I planned on having Carina taken back to NC and tortured for the shit she did. But with her basically admitting to doing some sick shit to Larissa made me snap. I shot the bitch between the eyes and watched her head split open before letting off a few more bullets.

Then I bent down and reached in Carina's back pocket for her phone. Whatever she was talking about wasn't getting into nobody else's hands. I wasn't gonna worry about the shit now when I still needed to find Larissa.

Larissa

This was the second time I woke up in the hospital after a traumatic situation. The first thing I asked the nurse was if she could call Messiah. I wanted him here with me. The doctor told me that I lost a lot of blood and also lost the baby girl I was carrying.

I was still unconscious when they removed my daughter from my womb. They asked if I wanted to see the baby and I refused. I was following all the stages of my pregnancy since I found out and knew that she would have been tiny but still was blinking, moving and had fingernails.

The feelings I was experiencing from the loss of my first daughter seemed more unbearable than anything I had ever experienced before. It was far worse than me and Messiah breaking up, being shot and even the physical abuse I suffered under the hands of Fe and Carina.

Thinking about those two caused a shiver to run down my spine. Images of being raped, violated and abused by that bitch and punk ass nigga replayed over and over in my mind. Carina was the real reason I lost my daughter. Her using the tool to hurt me caused my cervix to weaken and made the fetus' membrane rupture.

I heard the door to my room being opened and slowly lifted my eyelids back up with my attention now fully on the sound of footsteps. I hoped it was Messiah. I wanted his support and for him to mourn the loss of our daughter with me. Instead of Messiah I was unfortunately surprised when my mother and sister came in. I was fine with my sister Loraine being here, but wished she kept the shit to herself and didn't bring my mom.

I hadn't even seen or spoken to my mother, Greta, since the incident at her house with my step-father trying to rape me. She disappeared after that. The one time I tried calling her she told me she didn't want anything to do with me since I caused her husband to leave.

She didn't know that my boyfriend was the real cause of him being gone, or that the sick ass man she married was six feet under. I could only imagine how she would feel about that shit. But fuck her! She already turned her back on me. The only thing she gave me was life and for that I was grateful but that's as far as shit went for me.

I was wondering how either of them even knew that I was here. My question was soon answered when Messiah and my brother Enzo walked in together talking to each other like they had known each other for a while. I was really questioning what the fuck was going on.

After Messiah saw I was awake he rushed over to my bedside and leaned down placing gentle kisses on my forehead and cheek.

"How's our little man?" I asked referring to MJ.

My first thought when I woke up and learned that I lost the baby was how he was doing. I went with Fe in the first place to ensure our son's safety and would do that shit again even if I knew what would happen to me and my unborn if it meant MJ was kept safe.

"He's good. Maurice got him and mama's fine too." He answered, letting me know both MJ and Ms. Sheila were alright.

Knowing they were okay allowed me to feel some kind of validation for the shit that I endured. I reached down and touched my stomach out of instinct more than anything else and when the realization set in again that my daughter was gone, I looked up into Messiah's eyes. He bent forward and let his forehead rest against mine. While our heads were pressed together he stared back into my eyes. I let the tears flow.

"We're gonna be straight LaLa. I love you ma." He said just above a whisper so only I could hear.

He had so much emotion in his voice and I saw the tears threatening to fall from his eyes too. I knew then that he had talked to the doctor and knew that I lost the baby. He might not know everything I went through and I prayed he never found out but having him here with me, supporting me made me feel a lot stronger than I was. He wiped away my tears with his thumbs then stood back up.

"After you say your hellos and shit, I'm gonna need for ya'll to leave. She needs her rest." Messiah demanded.

He was only addressing my brother and sister with his statement. He didn't even look in my mother's direction. This was the man I loved, and he was doing what he did best taking charge and being the boss he was. I appreciated him for that. I loved my sister and brother and would love them to come back when I was up to it, but without my mother.

Messiah knew how I felt about both my parents so he was doing his best to protect me right now. I didn't even want her to speak to me to be honest. I felt like she had some kind of ulterior motive for showing her face now. My mother never gave a fuck about me, so there wasn't shit I wanted to have to do with her now.

Loraine and Enzo came over, gave me a hug and then said their goodbyes. I told them I would call them when I was released and we would get up with each other then. They said they understood. Before my sister left she whispered in my ear encouragement for me to hear my mother out.

56

My sister and brother were years older than me. They didn't understand why I was so hard on her. Truth be told both of them had better relationships with our parents than I did. Them being older caused them to have completely different childhoods than me.

I was the one who was treated like shit and discarded when it suited our parents. I already forgave them both but I would never forget the shit they did and the choices they made. My sister should have known better than to bring my mother here in the first place. She should have had my back.

I planned on having Messiah tell me more about how he knew my brother when we were alone. Neither one of us liked to discuss personal shit around outsiders or people we weren't close to. My mother was a stranger to me.

"Why are you here?" I finally asked when it was just me, Greta and Messiah left in the room.

"I came to check on you. Despite what you may think, I love you. I want us to have fresh start. I miss you." She responded.

"Let's be real. You don't care about me mom. You never have. I would rather us just keep our space." I told her.

I wanted to keep shit real with her. I wasn't the same girl I was when I first came down to NC looking for a relationship with her.

I didn't trust her ass further than I could see her. She put her husband before me, her own daughter. Now that I had a child of my own I could never understand that way of thinking and didn't even wanna try. No matter what pathetic reasons she had they weren't good enough.

From being with Messiah I was able to see what a real mother and child relationship should be like based on how his mama was always there for him. Shit, Ms. Sheila treated me better than my own mother did. So my attitude was fuck her. I had my family and she wasn't a part of it. I definitely didn't want her anywhere near my son. I would never subject MJ to being treated less than. If she was capable of it with me then I knew she capable of being the same way towards my son.

"Larissa you are being unreasonable. I made one mistake. I forgave you, so it's only right you forgive me." She pleaded her case.

The shit she was saying was just making me more mad. She really thought that she was doing me a favor by being here. Messiah must have realized that her presence wasn't doing nothing but upsetting me. That was something he wasn't gonna stand by and watch.

"It's time to go. My wife's straight. She's already got a family. You heard what the fuck she said. Now you gotta bounce." He spoke up on my behalf.

My mother looked back and forth between Messiah and me one more time before shaking her head as if she was in disbelief before she turned and walked towards the door.

"There will come a day where you'll wish I was in your life Larissa. I'm your blood and that means something. That man," She said pointing at Messiah, "will ruin you." She finished the last part and walked out of the door and out of my life for good I hoped.

I was released to go home a few days later and was still in some pain from the C-section they performed while I was out of it and first brought in. The pain I was experiencing was a kind of numb pain that went deeper than the physical shit that I had gone through or was feeling as I recovered.

Although I was more than ready to be home, I felt the loss of my daughter more as each day passed. MJ was the only bright spot for me right now. So I was trying to go back to school as soon as I could. I didn't want to be sitting around where I had time to think about all the possibilities I missed out on experiencing with my daughter now that I lost her. I would never even get to see her or hold her.

After coming home, Messiah asked me if I wanted to have a memorial service for her, but I refused. I thought it was best if we try and forget about me ever being pregnant. He told me he would take care of everything. Since we discussed it that one time we hadn't spoken on the topic again.

I wanted and needed to move forward. Even though we didn't talk about what happened, my heart was heavy with the loss of my child. The baby that was growing inside me was now gone and there was some things in life that you just couldn't get over all the way. I was struggling to even want to get out of bed in the morning and cried myself to sleep each night. The happiness I felt before the New York trip seemed like a distant memory.

I was recovering pretty well physically and was making progress in that aspect. I had been home for a week and during that time Messiah began to be gone more and more over the short course of time. Definitely more than he was before shit went down. It left me thinking that he had a problem with me or something which didn't help the depression I was already in.

Shit just wasn't normal between us. He came home every night and we talked every day, but we weren't our usual open selves with each other. I was sure it was each of us grieving in our own ways. I was trying not to think too much of it and figured with time we would find our way back to each other and back to the way we were before. Everything was still so fresh and the pain and loss we experienced was more than most people could bare.

The way I always dealt with shit was to keep going and push forward. I was determined to get my mind focused on other things and try not dwell on the shit that couldn't be changed. That was how I got through being discarded by my parents and that was all I knew to do to get past the situation I was in now.

This morning I woke up and finally decided to try and have a somewhat normal day. I called up Shanice and asked her if she wanted to go shopping and grab something to eat. She quickly agreed and made her way over to pick me up since I was still supposed to be taking it easy and my body was healing.

I didn't really feel like shopping but I needed to get the hell out of the house for a while since Messiah took MJ with him for the day. He always made time for our son and kept him close. He would take him with him to work sometimes and act like MJ was his sidekick. I was happy that he had his own strong bond with him that was separate from me. Messiah was the best father I could hope for.

After getting dressed in a comfortable track suit from VS, I threw my hair up in a ponytail and sprayed my body with my usual mist before turning off the lights to my room and heading downstairs. Shanice was already outside waiting for me. When she called I told her she didn't have to come in and I would just come out.

I walked over to her jeep and slid in slowly. After we spent some time looking around the mall stopping in a bunch of different stores I was ready to leave. I wasn't really in the mood to be shopping and Shanice could tell so she suggested we head over to the cheesecake factory to grab some food. So we left the mall and headed over to the restaurant.

We were lucky and caught the restaurant between lunch and dinner so it was pretty empty. I ended up ordering the fettuccini Alfredo and Shanice went for the soup and salad special. I ordered a drink too so that I could unwind some more before heading back home. Of course Shanice ordered a drink right along with my ass.

"Cheers bitch! To new beginnings. I know you goin' through it. But I'm here for you girl and you know I love your ass or whatever!" She said while holding up her drink waiting for me to clink mine with hers in a toast.

"Thanks, and I know it. I just can't seem to stop thinkin' about everything..." I confided in her.

"It's gonna take time. But you're one of the strongest women I know. The shit that happened to you was some of the worst shit a person could go through, but you got this sis." Shanice continued to reassure me.

"How can you be so sure? Shit just ain't right. Messiah and me just ain't right. I don't know nothing anymore." I said honestly.

I couldn't really explain how I was feeling. I was just in a funk. I knew the rationale behind it. That I had lost my child. That I had been through a traumatic situation. Maybe I was even experiencing some kind of PTSD. But the happiness and future I saw before shit went down, with my life and my family wasn't so clear any more.

Maybe me and Messiah would never have the happy ending I envisioned for us. Maybe the street shit would always end badly for me. I was the one who went through all the shit due to the illegal lifestyle Messiah lived. I wasn't saying it was his fault but when it was all said and done, I had been through some of the worst shit and all because of who I was with. Walking away from him wasn't an option for me. But it seemed like I was bound to live a life of pain with him too.

"Trust me. Things WILL get better. Just have faith." Shanice said.

I chose to end the conversation with that. There was no point trying to explain everything to Shanice when I didn't understand all the feelings I was having myself. We ordered one more drink with our dessert and of course their desserts were the best.

I was still glad to be out with my girl and was feeling a little better even if partially because the effect the alcohol was having on me. As we were getting our payments ready for the waitress to take up my eyes were drawn to the entrance of the restaurant.

Antoine was standing there with some bitch on his arm. He turned and saw me looking his way and then said something to the girl he was with before he walked in the direction of our table. My breathing picked up and my palms started sweating. I didn't want to be affected by Antoine, but I was. I loved my man. He was my everything. But I had history with Antoine. I never had any bad feeling towards him and felt bad for how shit played out between us, and then at the club when he approached me and all hell broke loose.

Even though he was sexy and I cared about him and probably always would a little I was with his brother and never would disrespect Messiah. I wished he would stop walking towards me and turn back around to go back to where his bitch was. It was better if we pretended like we didn't know each other.

Of course he didn't though. Instead he walked all the way over and stopped in front of our table looking down into my eyes. Not even letting his stare leave mine for a minute. He reached his hand out and placed it on top of mine on the table before saying,

"I'm sorry Larissa, for everything." Antoine said sincerely.

Tears welled up in my eyes and I put my head down. I couldn't stand to look him in the eyes any longer. I didn't want his pity or him feeling sorry for me. I didn't want anything from him.

"I appreciate that. But it's better if we don't speak." I replied.

"Look at me ma." He said.

I looked up at him and saw the love he had for me. It was written all over his face. But I loved another man more than I cared about him.

"You know I love you girl. I need to know was it mine?" He asked.

I continued to look up at him and shrugged my shoulders. The truth was I didn't know if the baby was his or not. Whether or not she was his didn't matter anymore though. She would never breathe her first breath, so discussing it was useless. Tears started streaming down my face and Shanice decided to speak up.

"Look, she's going through a lot right now. The last thing she needs is more stress. Please just leave her alone." She told him before coming over to my side of the table and helping me up with her arms wrapped around my shoulders. We walked out of the restaurant leaving Antoine and everything else behind.

When I got home, Shanice asked if I wanted her to come in with me and I told her I would rather be alone. I knew Messiah wouldn't be home for another hour or two and I needed to get myself together first. As soon as I was upstairs I filled the big ass tub in the master bath with water and stripped down. I needed to take a long hot bath.

Messiah

I was at Money Makers Inc. headquarters when I received a call from security letting me now Larissa was out to eat with Shanice. I was happy as hell she was getting out the house. When it was all said and done my baby was a fighter and she was gonna be straight. I knew she needed time. Shit both of us did to get past the loss of our daughter. I was also dealing with witnessing the shit those mothafuckas did to her, even though she didn't know I knew all the details. We hadn't spoke on the subject and I didn't plan on bringing it up.

But the part that pissed me the fuck off was that nigga Antoine dared to step to her while she was out to eat. That fuck nigga Antoine was spotted talking to her at the restaurant by the niggas I had watching her. As soon as word came through about that shit I was ready to murder the nigga. He knew to stay the fuck away from her. I told him back in New York that we needed to have a talk and I was ready to make good on that shit now.

I left immediately and headed over to my mama's to drop MJ off with her. She was completely healed and recovered from the shit that had happened to her too. After dropping him off I headed back out across town to the north side to meet up with Draco and Silk who were already on their way.

I already had eyes on Antoine's bitch ass and one of my security teams was posted out front of one of his traps on the north side where he was at. I was done waiting for the right time to get shit settled.

I made the decision to speak to the nigga first and see if we could come to some kind of understanding before I killed his ass. He was my brother but that wasn't the reason I hesitated to off his ass. He was backed by the Italians and since learning more about Larissa's brother's status in the Colombo family and Antoine's deal with them I didn't want to cause tension if it was avoidable.

The shit was close to home for LaLa and she didn't even know shit about that side of her family. I planned on telling her everything after things got better for her and between us. Right now we were going through a rough patch and I didn't want to cause it to be worse.

Truthfully, we were both dealing with the loss of our daughter and that shit hurt bad as fuck. We weren't talking to each other like we usually did, shit was just off at home. Thinking about how Antoine stepped to my damn wife and spoke to her had my blood boiling too. I didn't understood why he kept talking to her when he knew she was with me. He must have felt like he still had a chance or some shit. Larissa better not be giving his ass a reason to be chasing after her.

I parked my Audi and got out. The niggas outside were mean mugging me the whole damn time. I'm sure they already alerted that fuck boy I was out here, but they didn't put fear in my heart. I stood all ten and would fuck shit up whether I was one deep or not. Especially behind my family.

Draco and Silk pulled up next to me within a minute or two and they walked with me up to the trap like the mothafuckin' bosses we were. We didn't have our hands on our pieces yet but best believe them shits was ready and on hand if we needed them. Our security team was just approaching as we made it to the top of the steps and stood on the stoop.

The few niggas standing around that had been watching since I pulled up were grilling us still and all their conversation stopped. They knew who the fuck we were. They kept their eyes trained on us trying to be intimidating or some shit. Even though they were trying to play hard I saw the respect they had too. I had to give it to that nigga though, he actually had some killers with him and that said something about the mothafucka.

Antoine came out and stood there with his arms folded for a minute before he spoke up.

"The fuck you doing' here nigga."

"Fuck all that, we need to discuss some shit now." I stated.

He stood silent for a second and then turned around and walked back inside. I followed behind him with my niggas by my damn side.

There was a few folding chairs in the room so after the door closed I moved one so that it was facing the front door and then sat down clasping my hands in my lap. Draco and Silk moved the other chairs they were gonna sit in so that all three of us were positioned to see from all angles while keeping them in a circle. We weren't dumb enough to sit up here with the niggas who weren't on our team and not take precautions and be ready in case they tried some shit. We didn't come here to die. I came here to give this nigga an ultimatum. Either he was gonna stand down when it came to LaLa and keep his operation the size it was now without trying to expand. Or we were coming for him and his whole damn team.

Our organization now spanned the entire East Coast and normally small time shit that happened in any of the cities across the 8 states we had on lock would have been crushed the minute it popped up, but this was close to home and it was our own city so shit was different.

There shouldn't be no fucking problems on our home turf. This was still directly under our control. We liked to be hands on bosses here. We could have easily handed it over to our niggas overseeing shit last year and stepped aside when I became the plug, but this was home. It was only a matter of time before it was in our best interest to let this go too. Our operation and responsibilities were moving in another direction. When you came up from nothing to being the boss it was hard to let go of some things.

"So what the fuck you wanna discuss?" Antoine asked, getting straight to the point.

"I want you to keep your operation where it's at and not try and take over any new territory." I started before getting to the personal shit. "And I want you to stay the fuck away from my wife." I added not bulshitting around.

"Now why the fuck would I agree to do either of those things? I'm about my mothafuckin' money and want to build this shit up as much as possible. And your wife? Who? Last time I checked Larissa wasn't married nigga. She's grown as hell and if she wanna deal with me that's got nothing to do you with you." He boldly said.

I wanted to keep my cool with this nigga. He was saying shit trying to bait me into something and I needed to let shit play out. I came here to let him know what the fuck his options were. I told him what I wanted and now I was gonna let his ass know what would happen if he didn't.

"You really ready to go against me?" Think on that shit before you decide nigga. You know who I am and what the fuck I'm capable of. This shit ain't got nothing to do with you being my brother either. I could care less about that shit. I'll not only murder yo' ass, but every fuckin' person on your team and anyone else who's with you. I already got some of your so called niggas in New York ready to flip on your ass too. This ain't up for discussion. I'm telling you what's gonna happen."

"We'll see. I'm not some do boy nigga! What's in it for me to stay where I'm at? How I'm gonna bring in more dough and expand?" He finally asked good ass questions instead of acting like a little bitch. But the shit wasn't my fuckin' problem. Maybe things could be different if he wasn't the one nigga alive to fuck with Larissa, but he was. So it was what it was.

I didn't even like being in the same room as the mothafucka. I loved that girl too much and I wasn't about to sit up here with a nigga that felt my pussy. The thought of him talking to her earlier came to mind again and I was losing patience with the situation at hand. I came here and said what needed to be said.

"Not my problem. You ain't gotta give me an answer. I'll know if you agree by your actions. If you make a move on either area, you know what the fuck's gonna happen." I said as I stood to get up.

Draco and Silk got up ready to leave too. When we made that movement two niggas standing off to the side pointed and aimed their weapons at us. But we continued on our way walking up out of there like we fucking came in, without a damn problem. Those niggas knew we ran shit.

When I made it home it was already around ten. I went ahead and got MJ settled in his room before I even let LaLa know I was home. I wanted to talk to her about the shit that happened today and see where her head was at. I wanted to know exactly what the fuck her conversation with that nigga was about. I didn't like the thought of them holding a damn conversation.

That shit was suspect as hell and I couldn't stand to think that she was out disrespecting me. I was a selfish ass nigga and she knew exactly how I was behind her just like every other mothafucka did. She was my strength and my weakness.

Larissa was lying in bed in her red silk robe looking beautiful as fuck. She looked even better than the first day I saw her ass if that was possible. She still had another week before I could fuck though but the sight of her had my dick hard as hell. There wasn't shit I was gonna do about that though, there was no way another bitch was gonna be blessed with my dick again if I had my way. I wanted Larissa to become my wife. She was enough for a nigga like me.

I almost lost her not once but twice and knowing that I was the reason for her going through so much shit was still fucking with me. Just like it had been since she got shot behind my ass. I don't know if I deserved her and honestly I didn't know how we was gonna get past all the pain that came with being together.

I was a street nigga. It was all I knew. I couldn't give up the game and more than that I didn't want to give up the money or power that came with the shit. But it seemed like if I stayed in the game LaLa and my family would always be in danger.

I approached the bed and LaLa finally looked up from her kindle that she was reading on. She smiled at me which was something I hadn't seen since before she was taken and we lost baby girl. I still saw the sadness in her eyes and knew she spent time crying today just like she had all the other days since being home.

I couldn't return that smile though. I was still mad about having to go and check the nigga she fucked with in the first place. So instead, I sat down at the foot of the bed with my back to her while I took off my shoes. After unlacing them and setting them to the side I got to the point.

"What happened today with ol' boy?" I asked.

"What do you mean? I went shopping then out to lunch with Shanice. Nothing happened he said hello, that's it." Larissa said.

I could tell she was telling the truth but her tone was defensive which let me know right away there was more to the shit than she was letting on. Usually she didn't give a fuck if I questioned her, just like I didn't give a fuck if she asked me shit. We had been in a good place and never kept shit from each other from the beginning of our relationship, or so I thought.

I didn't want my woman to have feelings for another nigga. A man she fucked and what was worse was my brother, but I wanted to know for sure if she still had feelings for his ass. I don't know why I wanted to know but it was just something that I needed to hear.

"Why you so defensive if nothing happened? Let me know what's really good ma. You ain't never lied before so tell me this, you got feelings for that nigga?" I really wanted to know if she did.

To me if she held feelings for him, it was a type of betrayal. I never had feelings for any other bitch besides Larissa outside my family. Even when I did my dirt it wasn't no type of feelings involved towards the bitches. I already figured she cared about that nigga when we wasn't together and they was talkin' or whatever the fuck they were doing. But once we got back together that shit should have been dead. If she loved me like I loved her there wouldn't be room for anyone else to hold a piece of her heart.

"I love you Messiah, only YOU!" She said emphasizing the word you.

Yeah she was trying to reassure me. I knew she loved me that's not what I was questioning. She still hadn't answered my question and she was avoiding that shit. I wasn't about to ask her again either.

I got back up off the bed and walked out the bedroom without another word. I wasn't gonna beg her ass to keep shit real. She needed to boss up and let me know what was good. I wasn't gonna get played out even by the woman I loved. I wasn't a bitch ass nigga that let a bitch walk all over them.

When I asked for the truth that was what the fuck I expected to get. LaLa never acted like this before. Just like in the streets loyalty was everything. I was all the way in this shit with her and completely loyal since I fucked up after we first met. She was gonna have to be the woman I thought she was for us to continue the fucking conversation. I wasn't with the bullshit.

So I went downstairs into my office and decided to stay in there for the night. I would sleep on the couch down here. LaLa was gonna have to make shit right between us this time. And until she was honest about shit, I didn't wanna even talk to her ass.

Antoine

So what that nigga came demanding shit from me. I wasn't a bitch made nigga and would never cower away from a damn thing. I wanted to be smart about how I moved and the decisions I made though. I had niggas on my team that depended on the shit I did. That was the only reason I was considering that fuck nigga Money's ultimatum.

I was trying to think of a way to come out of the situation on top. It seemed like either way I was fucked. My number one priority was making bread. I could easily agree not to interfere with the shit he had going on with Larissa. I loved shorty but already knew her heart was with Money's ass. I wasn't gonna settle for a bitch that wasn't mine. Me staying away wasn't the problem.

The problem was I was still trying to expand my team and make more money. When that shit came out Money's mouth for me not to expand or he was coming after us, I honestly didn't know what the fuck to say.

I understood that me fuckin' his old lady was the real motive behind him wanting to kill my ass. Otherwise being that we were brothers could have worked to my advantage. I didn't know Larissa was his woman until after I met her ass and at that point she seemed worth it.

Plus he wasn't in the picture at all, at least I didn't think he was. Now I was looking at things from his perspective and understood why he wasn't willing to budge.

To him it looked like I came down here on some snake shit but that wasn't the case. I moved down to NC because my partna and best friend needed to get out of New York. When he suggested we move because we could make more money down south that shit sounded good.

Once I mentioned the shit to Enzo it was a done fucking deal. My damn connect was even more on board than I was. The Italians didn't have anyone down South pushing their shit. Me coming here didn't have shit to do with Money's punk ass. This shit was about my damn money. Not his feelings or his bitch.

When I saw Larissa at the restaurant I wanted to go over and speak because when Enzo told me she was five months pregnant I knew the child she was carrying could have been mine. We shared some good times together and no matter what I would always respect and care about her, even if we weren't together. She was good people and deserved the best even if she wanted to be with my dumb ass half-brother.

We still had a physical and mental connection and when I was around her the attraction was strong as fuck. Her pussy was still the best I ever had and I knew she loved my dick game. Even though shit went south after we fucked it wasn't because the sex. It was because her feeling's for Money. Shit, I bet she was fiening for my dick just as much as she did that nigga. But fucking with her would definitely cost me everything and I wasn't willing to risk everything for her.

I was gonna think of something to come out on top. I always did. So as I sat in my office at my club I let one of my favorite strippers do her thing while I leaned back in the seat and tried to come up with a plan.

The bitch was down on her knees under my desk and I was more than happy to let her give me some good ass head. She started moving her mouth faster until I let my nut go and busted while she sucked me dry. I didn't fuck with strippers like that so I zipped up my pants and patted her on her shoulder so she could get up.

My mind was set on one thing only and that wasn't a bitch. I was determined to come up with a plan. After shorty left the room and the door was closed I put in a call to Enzo and set up a meeting for tomorrow. I wasn't gonna sit back and wait for Money to make the first move. No matter who the fuck he was there wasn't no bitch in me.

Larissa

Two weeks passed since Messiah came in asking questions about my feelings for Antoine and we still hadn't had a real conversation about the shit. He got mad and walked out after I gave him an answer. He may not have believed what I said but the truth was I loved Messiah and only Messiah. I got defensive because I didn't want to tell him that I cared about another nigga, especially his own brother. It was a different kind of caring than what I felt for Messiah.

I was grateful to Antoine. He came in my life at a time when I was struggling to move forward and enjoy life again. He and I shared a lot of good times over the couple months we spent getting to know each other. We had so many conversations during that time about ourselves that I knew him pretty well.

I didn't want anything bad to happen to him and wanted nothing but good shit for his future. I didn't see us being together again and although the sex was amazing it wasn't the same as what I felt for Messiah and never would be.

I didn't want that nigga the way I wanted my man. Thinking about how bad I wanted Messiah had me horny as hell. I was cleared for sex last week but hadn't gotten any because we weren't on good terms.

I was still mourning the loss of my daughter and felt that shit every day. But with MJ and school I was able to push on. I looked at it like it wasn't meant to be and God knew better than I did. Sometimes we want things that aren't what's best for us. Some days were better than others. One moment I would be smiling and the next I would be feeing empty and grieving. No one could console me so I tried to stay positive.

This shit between me and Messiah wasn't helping either. I still had some animosity towards him too and couldn't help feeling like some of the shit that I had been through was his fault. I never was one to hold onto shit if I could help it, so that was another thing I was working to let go of. I wanted to be happy in life and everything I did have going on and going for me far outweighed the negative shit.

MJ's birthday was coming up at the end of the month. I was trying to stay more occupied and had been planning his party as much as possible in my free time. We were gonna have the party at our house which would be the first time we had a large group of people on the grounds. It was still gonna be only the people we could trust, so nothing too big. Family and friends only. Most of them already knew where we stayed even if they hadn't been over yet.

I just got home from school after picking MJ up from Ms. Sheila's and was in the living room on my laptop ordering the cake for his party. He was playing on the floor with some of his toys when Messiah came in. I was so horny and ready to jump on his dick it wasn't even funny. At this point I was willing to say whatever he wanted to hear just to get some dick. But my pride wouldn't let me make the first move.

Messiah must have noticed the way I was looking at him. Instead of saying anything he took an apple from the counter and bit into it being all extra and shit. He was definitely fucking with me and waiting until I made shit right between us. We were both stubborn as hell. After he took a big ass bite he wiped his mouth with the back of his hand and continued staring at me, with my eyes still trained on him too.

"Can we talk now?" I asked more as a plead than a regular question.

He chose not to respond to me and walked over to where Messiah Jr. was playing on the floor and sat down beside him. He started playing with him and ignored my ass like I wasn't even in the damn room. I rolled my eyes unintentionally. But his ass was really being petty now.

"Hold up lil man, I gotta get your mommy in check. She got all that attitude." Messiah said talking to our son about me.

I was pissed though. I wanted to be acknowledged and I needed some dick. So I got up off the couch and walked into the kitchen. Whenever I was frustrated cleaning was always my go to. It helped to alleviate my aggression instead of causing an argument or making things worse. I started to put the dishes away harder than usual when Messiah's ass walked over to where I was standing and wrapped his arms around me from behind.

Now he wanted to be all loving and shit but I was mad. When I asked if we could talk he was being petty. But the feelings he was causing to come over my body were persuading me to give in again. We were gonna have this talk regardless so it might as well be now so we could put it behind us. I was gonna be all the way honest with him, since that's what he wanted. I still didn't know how he was gonna take the shit but I was gonna do it anyway.

I turned around and he continued to hold onto me. We were inches apart and I felt his hard dick but I was still gonna discuss this shit so there was no more secrets between us. I wanted this to be the last time too.

"I meant what I said, I love you and only you Messiah." I started off.

Messiah backed up away from me and put space between us. He leaned up against the counter opposite of where I was standing. It was better that way so we could really talk with clear heads.

"I don't doubt that shit LaLa, but you need to tell me what the fuck that nigga got on you. It's obvious you got some kind of feelings for him." Messiah said back.

"It's not like you think it is. I care about him because when you and me wasn't together he came into my life and brought back some happiness that I didn't know I would ever experience again. I know you don't wanna hear this shit..." I stopped talking and turned away.

It didn't feel right to be confessing my feelings for another nigga. I couldn't even look at Messiah while I was saying the shit. It was a betrayal and I knew it.

"Keep going. I need to hear every fuckin' thing." He responded with a hard tone.

I knew he was mad as fuck. But I kept going like he wanted.

"When you left I was devastated. Antoine made me feel alive again and we shared all kinds of shit with each other. He was someone I came to depend on and there was feelings that developed. We spent a lot of time together. But now, it's not like it was for me. I don't have those same romantic feelings for him. I don't want nothing bad to happen to him, but I don't wanna be with the nigga." I finished.

Everything was laid out in the open now. It wasn't what Messiah wanted to hear but it was the truth. I cared about Antoine and always would. He was there for me, when Messiah wasn't and maybe that was what was fucking with him the most. It wasn't that I wanted to be with the nigga at all. He was sexy but he wasn't the love of my life. He wasn't Messiah.

Messiah moved his head from side to side and I could tell he was thinking shit over. I still saw the rage in his eyes behind the things I just told him and was waiting for him to say something.

"Come here." He finally said.

I knew he was done talking about the shit. A part of me was glad that the discussion was over. But I hoped what I revealed didn't do more harm than good for our relationship or for Antoine. I didn't want to be the reason he lost his life because after all he was a person who had been nothing but good to me.

I walked over to Messiah and he pulled me close and started kissing me deep and hard. Messiah loved with his whole heart and everything he did was demanding like the boss he was. When we made love it was the same way. I pulled back and started kissing on his neck while he palmed my ass and started squeezing it more while I whispered in his ear.

"I'm gonna put MJ in his room."

"Bet" Messiah said then slapped me on the ass causing me to jump a little.

He chuckled and then let me go so I could go get our son and put him down. I was more than ready for some makeup sex.

After making sure he was settled in and good I stopped in the bathroom down the hall from the master bedroom and got completely naked for my man. Then I went and walked into our room and saw Messiah laid back on the bed smoking a blunt. I got on top of him straddling his lap. He only had on his boxers and his body was turning me on even more.

Messiah was strong as hell and knowing he was all mine always did something to me. I really felt blessed to have him in my life and to be able to call him my own was the best feeling in the world. No matter how much shit we went through even almost losing my life, I was still happy with him. There was nothing like being connected to someone and having a deep love that conquered any other bullshit.

I reached out and grabbed the blunt from Messiah. I took a few pulls and coughed because it was some strong shit and I hadn't smoked in a minute. My coughing caused my breasts to bounce up and down and I guess that was enough for Messiah. He put the blunt out and started taking care of me.

He began playing with my nipples pinching and rolling them between his fingers. Then he cupped each one of them and squeezed. Him playing with my breasts made me start moving up and down out of instinct. He moved his hands to my ass and grasped each of my ass cheeks. I loved that shit even more. So I pulled at his boxers and moved so I could get them off of him. Of course his big ass dick was hard and standing at attention already. His dick was fucking perfect and the sight of it made my mouth water.

I wanted to really show Messiah how much I loved him and how everything I said downstairs about him being the only one for me was true. So I turned around and tooted my ass up in his face before I grabbed ahold of his dick. I started jacking it nice and slow and then deep throated it in one motion. As soon as the tip touched the back of my throat I opened my jaws wider and let it slide down more. Even after it caused me to gag some.

Messiah pulled my ass back into his face and I felt his tongue between my cheeks licking down to my pussy. He started flicking his tongue in an out of my pussy and ass. That shit made me go harder. I let the spit drip down his dick and moved faster to match the rhythm of his tongue. Me doing that shit caused him to stop for a second I guess from it being so good. I slowed down and started using my tongue while I sucked more.

He spread me wider than I even thought possible causing my pussy to be tight as fuck. He found my clit with his mouth and latched on. He started sucking on it and that was it for me. My body convulsed and I let my cum flood out while he tensed up and released in my mouth. After sucking him dry Messiah finally let up and stopped sucking on my clit.

He moved back and kissed and bit all over my ass before pushing me forward on the bed and getting behind me. I was on all fours when he slid his dick in. I was tight as hell and had to adjust to his size.

Once his big ass dick was all the way in he began moving in and out and rotating his hips with mine each time he was all the way in. I didn't know what the hell he was doing to me but I really couldn't take the shit. He was hitting my spot and causing me to scream out because it hurt so bad.

"Throw that shit back girl." Messiah said starting to talk nasty.

I always did whatever the fuck he said. So I started popping my ass making sure to back it up on him even more. He reached out and grabbed ahold of my neck from the back and applied some pressure. Him doing that shit caused my back to arch more than before.

He had me where I could barely fucking move and all that did was make the way he was fucking me better. His other hand reached around and rubbed on my clit. That sent me over the edge. I squirted all over and left a puddle under us.

Messiah went harder and faster. He pulled his dick out and flipped my ass around. Then he spread my legs wide into a scissor positon and entered me again. When he did that shit it was really like his dick wouldn't fit. His shit was too damn big and my pussy was clamping down.

"Take this big mothafucka, let the monster in shorty." Messiah said.

My juices started flowing after he said that.

"Fuck me, Messiah. Give me MY dick." I said back between moans.

He gripped both of my thighs and leaned forward into me. He had my ass where I couldn't move again and his dick was rubbing right on my clit from inside.

"Cum with me daddy." I said into his ear.

After that his body tensed up and mine started shaking. We both cummed together and then laid there afterwards until our breathing slowed.

"LaLa you know I love you shorty. On some real shit I'm sorry I wasn't there for you when you needed me. That shit's on me. We good now, can't shit come between us." He told me while his dick was still hard inside me.

I loved the way he felt inside me. I could never get enough of this man. It was like a weight was lifted off me with having told him everything there was to tell when it came to Antoine. I didn't want nobody by Messiah. He was right when he said nothing was gonna come between us.

"You ain't gotta apologize. Shit happens the ways it's supposed to. It only made us stronger together. And I love your ass more." I let him know.

I dozed off shortly after that. I was worn out from his dope dick. It was like a damn drug. There was nothing better than some makeup sex.

Messiah (Money)

It was the morning after me and Larissa made shit right between us. And I was back finally feeling like my usual self. Being on bad terms with her fucked with my head. I felt at my best when we were good. I learned that shit a while ago and I wasn't a nigga that made the same mistakes twice. I might fuck up in other ways, but when I learned my lesson that shit was it.

My son's first birthday was coming up and I was planning on making shit official with LaLa after his party. I was putting together something special for her since making her mine legally was something that I thought about constantly. I was already about to propose way back in Miami before all the bullshit happened with her getting shot and kidnapped, and now I was even more fucking ready.

My only hesitation came with not knowing what her feelings were for that nigga Antoine and the dangers that came her way because she was with a boss nigga like me. After she told me the complete deal between her and Antoine, I felt at ease about that shit. I still didn't wanna think about her fucking him or anything. But I had to give it to the nigga, he stepped up and took care of her when I wasn't around. I should be more upset with myself than her. I was the one who left her and gave another nigga the opportunity to step into her life. That shit would never fucking happen again either.

I wasn't gonna go back on the shit I spit yesterday and the ultimatum I gave his ass. But I wasn't really trying to kill his ass either. Me offing him would hurt Larissa so I wanted to avoid that shit. I would do anything for her so letting him live was something I could at least try and do for her. Some shit you go through makes you become a better person and when LaLa told me how he treated her and what they shared, even though I didn't wanna hear it, it showed me that I really shouldn't hold that shit against him for her sake.

I knew what she was telling me was the truth too. Me and Larissa were connected on a deeper level than the regular relationship was. We were in this shit for life. With the loss of our daughter and all the other ups and downs we had been through the fact that we were still together and in love was a testament to that shit.

When I left the house earlier I went ahead and picked up her engagement ring from the jewelers. That mothafuckin ring was nothing but the best. It was five carats with a yellow gold band. Larissa always wore gold jewelry and the diamonds were gonna make that shit stand out. I wanted every nigga and bitch to know I was her husband and she was mine.

My next stop was my mama's house so I could fill her in on the shit I had planned. Her and Larissa were close as hell and I wanted her input on how I could make the proposal even better. There wasn't a better feeling than having the two women you loved the most in the world having a close relationship. I don't think I would love LaLa as much as I did if the two of them didn't get along. Larissa was the perfect woman and there wasn't even a comparison for me.

When I pulled up in front of my mother's big ass house that she was now living in, there was two other cars parked in the driveway. My mama didn't have visitors or no shit regularly so that immediately caught my attention and made my guard go up. The cars were some luxury whips too. I had a feeling I knew who the mothafucka was inside with her and I wasn't gonna be happy about that shit if I was right. Even though my mama was grown and I was her son I was still protective of her.

I walked up the steps and onto the porch. When I opened the front door to the house of course exactly who I thought was there was the nigga who was inside. I stepped over the threshold into the house and came face to face with my damn father.

Emeri stood there dressed in some designer suit looking like an older version of me and my brothers combined. I had to give it to the nigga he kept himself in shape and looked younger than he really was. Just like my mother did.

When my mama noticed me come in her expression told me everything I needed to know. She acted caught up. She shouldn't have though. I told her to do what she wanted when it came to Emeri. This was her life and she could live it however she wanted. The problem was I didn't trust his ass one bit. I didn't want her to let him close and then for him to fuck her over.

Back in Belize Emeri was a hoe ass nigga and always kept a group of young bitches surrounding him. I didn't know what he was up to but I didn't have good feeling about the shit and my instincts were usually always right.

"Hello son." Emeri greeted me with a smile and his deep accent that I had grown accustom to.

I gave him a head nod in return and kept walking into the house over to the kitchen. Someone came walking down the hallway and I was wondering who the fuck the other person was over here. I knew one of the cars belonged to Emeri.

My brother Malik, who we called Biz, came into the kitchen catching me off guard. That shit surprised the hell out of me. It was just like his ass to get out and not say shit to anybody about it. He always liked to keep shit to himself. Just like how he didn't tell me about us having a damn brother out there. I wasn't mad though. That was how he moved out in the streets too.

He thought that if too many mothafuckas knew what you had going on there would be more problems. I couldn't say I blamed him for that because it was the damn truth. But even keeping shit on the hush didn't keep him from getting locked up. In the end his ass got popped anyway even with the caution.

I smiled wide as hell and greeted his ass.

"The hell you doin' nigga? When the fuck you get home?" I couldn't help but show my excitement.

It was good as hell to have my big brother home. Biz patted me on the shoulder and said,

"They got a new law and the shit changed my sentence. I'm glad to be back too. I'm ready to make shit happen." He said letting me know he was ready to get back to work.

He already knew that whatever I had going on, was something he could get in on. I would always look out for family unless they gave me a reason not to. Me and my brothers were close as hell and always had each other's backs. Just like how Maurice took care of my son while shit was bad in New York. I could always count on them two when shit wasn't right to come through, and that was how family was supposed to be.

After chopping it up with my brother for a little while I headed back out. I would talk to my mother later when Emeri's ass wasn't here. Even though me and him were technically on good terms, I didn't want any kind of relationship with him.

We had a talk about that shit back in Belize and he knew I wanted to keep our shit on the business level only. So fuck his feelings on the matter. I hoped like hell I was wrong about him being on some shady shit when it came to my mother.

The last thing I wanted was for her to get hurt. I also didn't want her to get too close to his ass because my plans were to still take him out and take over the cartel. If they were rekindling old shit, that was gonna pose a problem, but not stop what I wanted to do. I would just have to help my mama mourn and get over his death when it came to that.

It was time for me to head over to the businesses Money Makers Inc. was running around town. I wanted to stop by each one before meeting up with Draco and Silk later at headquarters. After I made it through all the businesses and was leaving out of the last one, it was just my fucking luck to come out of there and see the bitch Che standing by my ride.

Che's ass was posted up leaning against the hood waiting on my ass. I wasn't even thinking about her ass or the fact that she claimed to be pregnant by me since that shit first came out her mouth in New York. I'm sure she could see by the look on my face I wasn't happy to see her either. All this bitch meant was more problems for my home situation and that wasn't gonna fly with me. Not when me and LaLa were in a good place and I was about to propose. Whether Che knew that shit or not, she wasn't about to fuck anything up for us.

I stopped just short of the curb and put my hands in my pockets of my black joggers I was wearing. It was better if I kept my hands occupied so I wasn't tempted to strangle this bitch out here in broad daylight.

"The fuck you want Che?" I said in the mean ass tone I meant to use.

I wasn't for the games and she better watch how she came at me. There wasn't a doubt in my mind that she was on some real snake shit. There was so many bitches that tried pinning babies on me before I got with Larissa. The difference was that my patience was thin as fuck right now with the shit.

"Damn, daddy. I know you got your bitch, but I'm gonna be your baby mom too." She said with a hand placed on her stomach to emphasize that shit.

She might have gotten away last time at the restaurant with that shit, but I knew what the fuck I did with my dick. And I never fucked her ass raw. Not once. Even when she tried that slick shit, I never went for it. So her trying to pin her baby on me wasn't phasing me. We only fucked at my spot with condoms from my pack. I don't even know why I was wasting my time with this shit, since the baby wasn't mine. She better go find the real nigga who knocked her ass up because it wasn't me.

"Get the fuck on. And I would check you 'bout calling my wife a bitch but you ain't even worth the effort. On the real, me and you both know that baby ain't mine shorty. I strapped up every time I fucked." I said as I started moving toward my car door.

I spent enough time entertaining this bitch. It was time to meet up with my niggas and she was holding me up.

"But the baby is yours Money. I put holes in the condoms. I love you. I'm willing to keep quiet." She said.

She started getting emotional with tears in her eyes and her accent started really coming out more making it hard to understand her last words. I ignored the shit she was spitting and hopped in my ride. She got the message and took her ass on, off the hood of my ride before I backed up and then peeled out.

While I was driving over to our headquarters the shit she said kept replaying in my mind. I hit the steering wheel with the palm of my hands a few times mad as fuck. If what she was saying was true it was really gonna fuck with Larissa's head. Especially now that she just lost our daughter. I wasn't about to put this shit on her and have that stress added to her grieving. Not when we were just getting past it.

If the baby was mine, I would without a doubt step up and be a father. I didn't know how I would make it work but I would. My whole mood was fucked up by the time I pulled up to our building. I needed to get my head together because the meeting we were having was to discuss Biz coming back in and also plans for my proposal to Larissa.

What started out as a good ass day turned out to be fucked up. My brother getting out and being home was the highlight by far. Otherwise shit was wild. That shit with my mama and Emeri was way too fucking close for comfort. And Che fucked up shit even worse. It was like one step forward and two back.

I hoped everything worked out in my favor in the end. But it seemed like there was always something coming against what me and LaLa were trying to build.

Shanice

Today was my nephew's first birthday and I was helping Larissa with last minute errands. We had been planning this shit for the last month or so really doing the most. Every time she came up with an idea I added to the shit. There was no such thing as too much when it came to that little boy.

MJ really was the best baby and was something else. He was definitely a hand full and was for sure taking after his damn daddy with his attitude. But he loved him some aunty Neesy. In my eyes he could do no wrong.

His birthday was gonna be nothing but the best. Larissa decided on a sesame street theme. Her and Messiah always pushed the educational shit. In our circle we didn't really fuck with any dummies that was for sure. So MJ stayed watching PBS and for a one year old he was way advanced. I swear it was like he could talk in phrases already and shit.

I let Larissa drive today because Silk put my car in the shop to have a tune up and oil change. He always took care of my ass. I never had to worry about shit with him and the small things showed me how much he really cared about me. He never wanted me to go without or have anything other than the best of everything.

A couple weeks ago I met his daughter for the first time. I thought I was gonna hold some kind of ill feelings towards her and that was why I pushed the shit off for as long as possible. The last thing I wanted to do was treat a child bad, especially Silk's. I also knew for me and Silk to really last I was gonna have to step up and be a good step parent to his daughter Kenedra.

I shouldn't have even worried about the shit though. She was absolutely adorable and from the time I first held her I knew that I was gonna be fine with the situation. It wasn't her fault that her parents didn't work out. It wasn't like she was created during a time that Silk stepped out on me or anything. She was beautiful and I could already see myself helping to raise her as if she was my own.

I still was nowhere near ready to have my own kids though. I wanted to get done with college and start my career. I was expecting a damn ring and a wedding before I popped any babies out of this pussy. Not that there was anything wrong with those women who chose to have children without being married, but I never even saw myself with kids to begin with. After Deandre I really never thought shit like a happily ever after would even be in the cards for me. But then I met Kenneth "Silk" Wallace.

He was my knight in shining armor. That shit I didn't expect or knew existed all into one. My hood fairytale. I still remember the first time his cocky ass approached me, down to the cologne he was wearing even though that was well over a year ago.

Larissa pulled into a parking space outside the party supply store. This was our last stop before heading back to her house and getting everything ready. We were gonna be back around noon leaving us a few more hours to finish decorating. Then I was gonna head home too to get ready.

She was having the party catered by Buffalo Wild Wings so food wasn't something we needed to worry about. But all the other shit we came up with in planning MJ's first birthday was nothing to play with. I knew we really outdid ourselves, but his first birthday only came once.

The store was pretty dead just like most of the other places in the strip mall where we were at. It was still early as hell on a Saturday morning. Shit it was only ten thirty. I was wearing some leggings and one of Silk's sweaters. It was still cold, but not too bad for February. I was never a morning person but me and Larissa each got big ass coffees extra-large when we first headed out for the day. There was no way I was allowing her to do all this shit by herself. That was what best friends were for.

After grabbing some more balloons and getting them inflated we headed back to the house. There wasn't even anymore room left in Larissa's SUV for another damn thing.

"Girl who the hell keep texting your ass back to back? I know it's not Silk's ass 'cus your ass would've answered." Larissa questioned.

She had a point. If it was Silk texting me I would've answered the shit. But it was nobody but stupid ass Deandre. Since the day he first tried getting in contact with me I had been ignoring his ass. I mean the nigga even showed up to my parents' house according to one of his messages and tried asking me why I wasn't there. He was starting to be on some real stalker shit. I didn't want to tell Silk about it because he would over react and probably kill him. I didn't want shit to go that far over him just trying to talk to me.

I wasn't trying to get my ass killed by Silk either and the more he continued trying to get ahold of me, it made it seem like I had some shady shit going on when that wasn't the case at all. I decided to come clean and tell Larissa about everything. Even though me and her didn't know each other when me and Deandre was together, I told her everything about my past including my relationship with him.

Deandre was always my weakness just like an Achilles heel. He really brought out the best and worst in me. I swear when we were together he got me to do shit I would never think of doing now. He introduced me to a whole different lifestyle.

When I first got with him I was innocent to a lot of shit. He had me targeting niggas and hitting licks with him. I was willing and ready to do whatever he asked me to do. If he needed a place to stash his dope, I put that shit on me and hid it while being searched. There was no limit to what I would risk for the love of that nigga.

The thing I realized when he was locked up and came to my senses was that no real ass nigga, that's a true man would ever let his woman take any kind of fall for the shit he was doing. Deandre was a true bitch in the streets. I remember one time being stopped by an undercover unit and he asked me to hide a few rocks for him. Of course being the dumb little ass girl thinking I was grown, I did it without hesitation.

There was only a male officer so they couldn't search me. We were both handcuffed and they tried to scare the shit out of us. I held firm and stood tall through that shit. Thinking back on it now, I was only sixteen fucking around with a grown ass man and was naïve to most of the shit he had me involved in. My whole future could've been fucked up behind him and he wouldn't have given a fuck.

Then when I found out he got a bitch pregnant it ended up opening up my eyes to the shit for what it really was. He didn't give a fuck about me. He cared about what I was willing to do for him.

So at this point I didn't have a single thing to say to that nigga. I wanted him to leave me the fuck alone. At the end of the day I was glad that I met him and learned a lesson from being with him. There was a time that I loved him more than I loved myself. That was why I was hesitant to give Silk a chance to begin with. But now that turned out to be the best decision I could have made.

Silk pushed me to succeed in everything I did. He was a constant motivation and the support I felt from him alone was something I never experience with Dre. Not that I was trying to compare the two or anything. But the shit was completely different.

"It's my ex. His ass keep trying to talk or some shit. I'm not with it at all. I can't shake his ass for nothing. The nigga showed up to my parents' house and everything girl. I'm not trying to get Silk into my shit." I confessed to Larissa.

She hit me with some real words of wisdom.

"Bitch you better tell your man about that nigga. If it's one thing I know from experience shit always comes to the light. Plus if that man don't mean you no good, Silk needs to handle his ass sooner than later."

"But you know how our niggas are... One word to Silk and Dre will be six feet under. I'm not trying to be the cause of his death."

What I was saying was the truth too. I knew exactly the type of men we were with. There wasn't a doubt in my mind that Silk would handle the shit. But I didn't want Dre's death to be on my conscience. At one time I loved him and even though he pulled all kinds of bullshit on me, I would always look at him as my first love. I saw Dre as part of my past that helped shape me into the woman I was today. I didn't hold any grudges because everything happened for a reason.

"I get that girl. That's the same way I feel towards Antoine. But he wasn't a fuck nigga who did me dirty either. From everything you told me Deandre was always up to some shit, and he always had you in jeopardy while you was together. He can't be trusted and I don't want anything to happen to you because of his ass. You need to tell Silk. But it's up to you on whether you do or not. Just think about it at least."

"I will." I said ending the conversation.

I still wasn't planning on telling Silk. If it came down to it and Deandre continued to pop up and try and get up with me, maybe I would. But for the time being I was gonna handle the shit myself.

I looked back down at my phone and starting reading through all the messages Dre sent me so far. Larissa must have understood that I was done with the topic of conversation because she turned the music back up and we just vibed out the rest of the way to her house.

As we pulled into her long ass driveway I decided to go ahead and take the bull by the horns and take the initiative to handle the shit with Dre. It was obvious that he was persistent and not gonna leave me alone until I had whatever conversation he was talking about. I figured once I saw him face to face I could really let him know that there was nothing more between us and that I had a nigga. It was gonna be my last attempt of handling the shit before I told Silk. If he still didn't get the message then I would bring Silk into it and let him handle Deandre.

I shot him a quick text telling him we could meet up later tonight at my parents' house. Deandre was cool with all my family from my stuck up parents all the way down to my cousins. Him and my cousin Brian used to real tight back in the day. That was how I met his ass in the first place.

My cousin Brian was still missing since around the same time Torio pulled that shit on Money. Word was that he was on the run from Money and his team, but I didn't believe that my cousin was a snake. So I never brought the shit up to Silk or asked him about it. Brian was my family and was the person who taught me a lot of shit about the streets. I didn't want to think the worst of him. He also was the person who always lived by the code of not being a snake or a snitch, so it was hard to believe.

After the text was sent I stuffed the phone back into my purse and got ready to help Larissa bring in all the shit we bought for the party. Fuck that, I was gonna call Silk and have him, Draco and Money come out when we pulled up so they could carry the shit in. That was what men were for.

Larissa

It was the day of MJ's first birthday party and I was on cloud nine. I swear this party felt like a complete new beginning for our family. This was the first celebration we had ever had period. Me and Messiah had been together for almost two years and although time was flying by, we really had gone through a bunch of shit.

Losing our daughter was another reminder of how short life truly was. I realized that shit after nearly dying when I was shot by Carina, but it's easy to get caught back up in life and lose sight of the fact.

I was grateful for Shanice's help in getting everything ready for the event. She always was there for me and was the best aunt I could ask for with MJ. Even though we weren't blood you couldn't tell me that. She did more for me than my own blood so she was family.

When she told me that fuck nigga Deandre was trying to get in contact with her to the point of becoming damn near a stalker I tried to talk her into telling Silk. I knew that secrets had a way of coming to the light and no relationship could survive them. Secrets caused mistrust and she should know that firsthand with going through it when Silk kept shit from her.

But more than anything I had a feeling that Shanice's ex was a danger to her. She told me all about the shit he had her into when they were together and she was only sixteen. My friend was as thorough as they came and was the definition of a down ass bitch. It wasn't just that he cheated on her that gave me that feeling. He really was a no good nigga.

Any grown ass man that got with a young girl and had them do their work to make money and fill their pockets alone was downright shady. I tried to talk some sense into her but she was her own person and could make her own decisions. I hoped that she didn't regret not telling him later.

The party was getting ready to start any minute. I invited my brother and sister. I wanted them to get to know my son and be a part of both of our lives. We always were close to each other growing up. They both were my protector since I was seven years younger than my sister and ten years younger than my brother. We just grew apart once they were old enough to move out. Right after my sister turned eighteen my parents split up and then everything changed for me. But it wasn't their fault that our parents turned their backs on me.

I wasn't even mad at my mother or father anymore. What happened in the past was in the past. I was happy with the woman

I was and understood that going through shit was what helped me to become who I was. Hopefully going forward after today we would all be able to spend more time together.

Enzo lived up in New York and Loraine lived back in Chicago. So them making the time and preparations to be here for the day meant a lot.

I went over to the stove and turned it on the warm setting so the wings and hot sides I ordered would stay warm while everybody was arriving. I had the entire entryway, living room and kitchen decorated with a Sesame Street theme. MJ loved to watch Big Bird and Elmo. He was so smart for his age and would even try and count along with the show. There were balloons spread around and he was playing with one of them. A damn balloon was better than a toy to him.

Messiah came into the kitchen and walked up in front of me. He stood across the island staring at my ass like the weird ass nigga he was. But my man was still the sexiest nigga alive.

We took our family pictures about a half hour ago with the photographer that we booked. All three of us were wearing coordinating colors of white and accented red. Even MJ had on a white matching polo shirt with red Jordans. Messiah was looking like a damn snack turning me on with his sexy ass dreads, fitted and gold jewelry. My panties were wet for real. I couldn't even look at his ass without being turned on. Even at something like our son's birthday.

Messiah's ass was too damn cocky too, because he knew exactly what I was thinking. He leaned back after snatching a chip and eating it and shrugged his shoulders with a big ass smirk plastered on his face.

"All you got to do is say the word ma. You know I got you. You ain't gotta stare a nigga down if you want the dick." He said in his usual matter of fact way.

"Whatever. You ain't all that." I responded right back playing shit off.

His attitude was always too much even if he was right. He walked around the island and came up behind me where I was still standing. Then grabbed onto my hips and pressed me up against his body. I instantly felt his big ass dick that was rock hard. That wasn't doing nothing but turning me on more and we were expecting people to arrive any minute.

I tried to back up and get back to tending to the last minute shit, like getting drinks out. But of course Messiah wasn't having that. He could never stand to not have the upper hand and be the boss that he was. So he held me right the fuck where I was not letting me move away. He was so damn strong I couldn't even move against his strength.

He brought his other hand down and cupped my pussy through my jeans. He started rubbing on me through the fabric and caused my whole body to tremble from that shit. I closed my eyes unintentionally from the good feelings he was giving me. Then his ass stopped and roughly turned me around and started kissing me.

This man was my damn weakness. His hands started working their way up under my shirt when the doorbell rang. I took that as our cue to stop. So I tried pulling away again. But Messiah was still being stubborn. He continued to rub on my breasts like he didn't just hear somebody at the damn door. I finally was able to break our kiss enough to plead my case.

"Messiah we got company bae. Let me get the door." I said.

"I want some of my pussy. Fuck 'em." He told me back.

"Please. I got you later daddy." I said again leaning into him some and grabbing his dick through his pants.

Messiah could never say no to me. So he was just gonna have to deal with a hard dick that I would tend to later. I wasn't gonna mess up our son's birthday. Messiah never gave a fuck about anything when it came to dicking me down.

He didn't care who was around, where we were or who it inconvenienced. He really was that nigga. I loved that shit though. But right now he would have to wait. I'm sure he would make me pay for the shit later.

He let me go get the door and I knew he was adjusting his dick and trying to get his mind focused on something other than fucking me. He had such a big dick that even when it wasn't hard you could easily make out the print through his pants. I went ahead and got MJ and brought him over to him before finally opening the door after the doorbell sounded for the third time.

It was Shanice and Silk. Draco came in right behind them and I decided to leave the door open with the screen closed so people could come right in without having to wait for me to get the door. I had everyone go into the living room. There really wasn't any other kids in our circle of friends or family except for Silk's daughter who was a little older than MJ.

Silk brought her over for the party and Shanice was doting on her like she did with any other child she took care of. I was proud of my friend for being willing to step up to the plate and play the step parent role. That wasn't easy and most of the time even when the person said they would treat the child like their own, it didn't' even up happening. Most step parents weren't shit and I knew that from experience. But Shanice was different. I saw the love she already had for that little girl.

Drinks started flowing and people were talking while the babies played on the floor. The adults had wine and liquor to choose from and I already had one glass of wine but nothing more since I was still the hostess. My sister and brother finally arrived and as soon as they came inside I gave them each a hug.

Everyone was enjoying themselves and I was finally able to sit back and relax once we had dinner and cake. Shit was just a good ass vibe. MJ opened all of his presents which took a damn hour in itself because he was so damn spoiled. Kenedra helped him open them and the two of them together were really a sight to see.

At first MJ didn't want nothing to do with her and wouldn't share anything. But after an hour or so he was following her around and giving her everything he had. I was thinking that he was really gonna be a damn ladies' man just like his daddy and couldn't do nothing but shake my head at the thought.

MJ and Kenedra were tired so me and Shanice put them down to sleep upstairs in his room. When we made it back downstairs I was surprised to see my sister and Draco booed up in the corner of the living room. My sister was beautiful as hell but Draco was young and wild so it was an unlikely match.

I shrugged my shoulders and went over to where Messiah was sitting and plopped myself down right on his lap. He wrapped his arms around me while resting his chin on my shoulder. This was one of the best moments we had since living here. There was nothing like being surrounded by family and that's what we all were.

The doorbell rang and I was wondering who the hell it could possibly be. Everybody that was somebody and who was invited was already here. Me and Messiah both had been lax with the security footage since we were having a party. So I scooted off Messiah's lap and looked at him with a questioning look.

He looked pissed off like he knew some shit was about to go bad. He immediately stood up and made his way over to the door. I was left wondering what the hell was going on. Nobody else even knew where we lived beside the people in the room or so I thought.

Silk and Draco must have been thinking some shit was off too, because they followed right behind Messiah. I stayed right where I was at until I heard the voice that was coming from the door.

Messiah

Here I was enjoying my fucking family and then this nigga showed up at my damn house. Nobody should even be able to get past security so the fact that his ass was on my porch knocking on my door was pissing me the fuck off.

My niggas were right there with me when I opened the door. All three of us pulled our guns out and had them aimed at the mothafucka. Antoine's bitch ass stood there like shit was all good when I moved closer with my shit still drawn and targeted at him.

I had to give it to the nigga he must be my brother because there was no fear in his eyes and he seemed relaxed. This was the second time I pointed my shit in his face and he didn't flinch. There was no other nigga still living that I had pulled a gun on and not used the shit on. He must have a guardian angel or I was becoming soft.

"The fuck you doin' at my house nigga?" I said loud as hell.

I wasn't one to even talk that much but this nigga coming here was more than disrespect. We weren't nowhere near cool or no shit and he better have a good ass reason for bringing this shit to my home.

This was a day of celebration. For my son's first birthday and also because I was gonna propose to LaLa later at our spot. The last thing I wanted was for this nigga to be here.

"I thought you would want to know I got that nigga Fe. My team has him and they're waiting on word from me to make a move." His ass said.

Fe got away while we were in New York. I took care of Carina's ass on the spot but there was no fucking trace of his ass. At least Antoine was here for a good reason and brought this to me personally. He knew exactly what the fuck Fe did to Larissa and how he caused her to lose the baby. He didn't know all the details and neither did anyone else alive except for me and that nigga Fe.

I watched the sick ass video Carina took of them two mothafuckas raping and torturing her while she lay there helpless. The shit made me sick to my stomach and when I watched it I threw up everything I ate. I erased it and then destroyed the phone. I never wanted anyone else to see that shit.

I never told LaLa I saw it either. I didn't want her to think I looked at her different for the shit she went through. I felt worse knowing that she had to endure all that because of me. She didn't' deserve none of that shit. That was just another reason why I was so set on making sure she was taken care of for life. I would give her anything in the world she wanted.

Antoine telling me he had Fe did alleviate some of the tension in the room so I lowered my weapon. But I was still on ten about how the fuck he made it on my property without security intervening. My team kept fucking up when it came to my family's safety. Which was my number one priority even more important than making money.

"Why you bring this to me? What's in it for you nigga?" I asked.

I knew there was a reason he was giving me this information and bringing Fe's ass within my reach. I'd been after that nigga for a minute now. There had to be a reason more than just doing me a favor. There was no love lost between the two of us.

"I want a truce. I'm not gonna go against you on either front. You set the terms, but I wanna be able to expand to other states as long as it don't fuck with your operation without problems." He explained.

"And if I say no. The fuck you gonna do nigga?" I came back with.

"Then I'll handle the nigga without your involvement. I'm not trying to step on your toes here. But I'm a nigga about my money and me and my team are gonna eat." He responded.

I stood there thinking for a minute. Draco and Silk still had their shit pointed at

Antoine. I turned to each one and nodded my head. Both of them lowered their heat but kept the shit at their sides. I understood their caution. Our loved ones were inside. Even though Draco didn't have an old lady he was still family. He was a thorough ass nigga and he proved that he was the same loyal partner I started this shit with.

"Alright. This how it's gonna go. You got your truce but I'm a hold you to everything you just said nigga. I won't tolerate nothing else." I said referring to the street shit and Larissa. Fuck the fact that he was my brother. That shit was a technicality only. "I'm gonna have Draco and Silk meet you at a set location where you can hand that nigga over. Don't try no funny shit. I'm not making no more threats nigga" I finished.

I would have to wait to take care of Fe until later. But at least my niggas could get him from Antoine's boys and take him to the warehouse. I was gonna make Fe really regret the day he ever decided to go against me, and even more all the shit he did to my wife.

Thinking about Larissa was the only reason I was staying calm right now. I wasn't gonna put nothing before the shit I had planned for her tonight. I already copped the big ass diamond and had our spot ready for me to finally boss up and ask her to be my damn wife. In my eyes she was already my wife, but making it official was something that would bond us for life legally. More than that I believed in that two becoming one shit.

I was a street nigga but when you had a down ass rider on your team, there's nothing in the world that compared to that shit. I was the luckiest nigga alive to have found LaLa and blessed to be able to call her mine.

Draco and Silk went ahead and said their goodbyes to everybody. Antoine was on his way back out the front door. He was only inside the foyer but when I turned back to walk into the living room I saw Larissa's expression and knew she figured out who was here. She had a look of concern. But that shit didn't affect me the same way it would have before we had that talk.

Now I understood that her concern came from a different place than I was thinking it was. She was a good person and didn't want him dead. Other than that, I realized that I was the only one who had her heart. When I said I would do anything to make her happy that included letting that nigga live.

That was another reason I agreed to the truce. I could have easily scooped Fe up from his team since they were a small time operation compared to everybody I had with me. But it was better to leave shit be and that way I wouldn't go against what LaLa wanted and still get to kill Fe's ass anyway.

LaLa noticed the tension on my face and that wasn't what I wanted her to be thinking about. So I relaxed more before I got closer and gave her a smile. She smiled a sexy ass smile back at me making me think back to the shit we were about to get into before the guests arrived earlier.

I reached out my hand for her to take while she was sitting on the couch. It was time for us to say our goodbyes and for me to man up.

"We appreciate ya'll coming. We're 'bout to bounce. Shanice you good?" I finished by asking Shanice if she was straight. She had already agreed to stay with the babies and close up the house after everyone else left.

When I said that I planned for everything, I didn't miss a beat. Larissa looked at me questioningly and then asked,

"What the hell you up to Messiah?"

"No questions ma. I got you." I said and then pulled her hand up so I could kiss the back of it.

Her body always responded to me and she shivered from my lips brushing against her skin. She knew exactly what my mouth was capable of. Her pussy would have to wait though because I was on a mission.

I went over to the garage and held her hand the whole way over to our ride. I opened her door for her so she could get in and even though I'm sure she was dying to know what the fuck was going on and what I was up to, she just went along with the shit. Larissa hated surprises or so she said but she always got excited with the shit I did for her.

It was dusk and the sun was setting when we turned into the path that led to our spot. She recognized the place and turned to look over at me with a smile on her face. This place was special to us.

It was the first spot I took her ass to when she put her trust in me when we had just met. This was the same place that we reconciled at after I fucked up and it was just something about us two being here that was some fate shit. I wasn't a romantic nigga but for LaLa I made an effort to show her how much I loved her and that she was my queen.

As soon as we made it to the clearing her eyes started watering and tears flowed freely down her face. She wasn't crying those sad tears I had seen too many times already, but these were out of joy. That made me feel like I was doing something right.

She hadn't even got a good look at everything I set up yet since we were still in the whip. I already knew LaLa was gonna say yes. My nerves were about getting everything right and making this good enough for her. I was a perfectionist and she was fucking perfect. I didn't wanna fuck this up like last time.

The trees had lanterns hanging in them with candles burning. I set up a small white table in the middle of the opening between the tall overhanging tree branches. There was one white chair next to the table and three objects on top of it.

I turned off the engine and got out of the car. I walked over to Larissa's door and opened it for her. She wiped away her tears with a tissue and then grabbled ahold of my hand. I led her over to the chair and had her sit down before saying a word.

She immediately noticed the objects sitting on the table and took her time looking at each one. The first item I had for her was a keychain. It had the date engraved in the gold setting that I first saw her. The keys represented how we met. It was a gift for our past. She set the keychain back down after running her hand over the engraving. It was all gold with a heart on the end that had the date on one side and on the other side read "You're my heart" It was short and to the point.

Others might look at me like a bitch going all out of the way for my woman. But that was what real niggas did. I wouldn't bow down to any other mothafuckas alive, except Larissa. She could get it all.

Once she placed the keychain back on the table she moved on to the next object in the middle of the other two. The shit she was looking at now was for our present. It was a picture of me, her and MJ that was taken today before the party.

I paid the photographer extra to have that shit printed and brought here. The picture was placed in a sterling silver frame. The frame was top of the line and had our family name "The Lawson's" on the top above the picture. Her tears started back up and she looked up at me.

"Thank you Messiah. You didn't have to do all this, but I love it."

"You got one more ma. This one's for our future." I replied back.

The third gift was wrapped in a box. She went ahead and opened the wrapping and then carefully pulled the box out. It was like she didn't want to break anything. Once she got the lid off the box she saw two things inside. She pulled out the brochure first.

The brochure was of a vacation resort in Belize. We were heading there tomorrow for our wedding, but she didn't know that yet. She saw the reservation dates and started getting all excited.

"Messiah! Oh my God I don't even have a passport and what about school?" She started asking with excitement.

"Open the other one La." I stopped her questions.

She looked back down and saw the ring box. Her hands started shaking and once she picked the box up I dropped down to one knee and took the ring from her. I said all the shit that I was feeling.

"You're my other half, the best thing that's ever happened to me. I'm a street nigga and I never thought I would love anyone the way I love you. You got a nigga Larissa. Will you marry me?" I asked while looking in her eyes.

She started shaking her head up and down and had her hands covering her mouth from all the emotions she was feeling.

"I wanna hear that shit girl." I said lightening the mood.

"YES! Messiah I love you so much. YES!"

"Good 'cus we're leaving for Belize tomorrow and making that shit happen right away. Everything in that box was a representation of our future. That shit starts right now." I told her before standing back up and pulling her up with me.

We stood there and kissed for a few minutes until it was time for me to get back focused on the next shit I needed to handle.

Usually I would be ready to fuck right here and now. But Fe needed to be handled first. Larissa probably could tell something else had my attention now that the proposal happened, but I wasn't gonna bring that shit up to her. The last thing I wanted was for her to have to think about the bad shit that happened to her.

We drove back to the house. She was happy and had a permanent smile on her face. But we both knew each other well enough to know when some shit was up. Once we were parked outside our home she spoke on that shit.

"Whatever you got going on that had Antoine over our house I don't want you to keep from me. I can handle whatever it is." She said bossing up on my ass.

"I'm not trying to put this shit on you though. It's my job to protect you." I answered her.

"What happened to trusting me enough to let me in on the shit you got going on? I'm not as weak as you think. I been through enough shit, and it's only made me stronger. So what's up?" She asked again.

Shit I wasn't trying to tell her but I also wasn't about to start keeping secrets from her and shit. I didn't want to do that shit and then later on it turn into something else. So I decided to go ahead and fill her in on what was going on.

"That nigga came by because he found Fe. He made a deal with me to turn him over and he gets to live. Right now, I'm headed out to the warehouse to handle the mothafucka." I revealed.

Larissa didn't say anything back for a few moments. Then she said some shit that should have surprised me but it didn't. I knew exactly what she went through at the hands of that nigga.

"I'm coming with you. I'm ending that nigga's life." She said in a cold hard voice.

This was the other side of Larissa. The side I saw in my office when she capped Chyna's ass. But now her voice seemed even more ruthless. I understood why it was important to her that she was the one to off the nigga, more than she even knew. So I agreed to let her come with me. We didn't exchange any more words on the subject. I just put the car in drive and pulled back out of the driveway headed in the direction of the warehouse.

LaLa and me both were zoned out for our own reasons on the ride. So I turned up the music and blasted that shit. I looked over and saw that Larissa was getting ready to light up a blunt. My baby didn't even smoke like that but always kept some shit on her. I didn't say shit, but took the blunt and lit it up for her. After a few pulls I handed it back and let her do her thing.

After the hour drive up to our warehouse we both jumped out of the whip ready to make shit happen. Even on the way inside my thoughts got sidetracked watching LaLa's sexy ass walk in front of me. I was ready to see her boss the fuck up and was confident that she was gonna handle this shit like a pro. That shit had my dick hard as fuck, so I adjusted myself before I stepped inside behind her.

As soon as we were inside Draco and Silk both looked at us with surprised looks on their faces. Even though I told them about how Larissa handled shit with Chyna they didn't really believe that shit. They never witnessed nothing but the sweet and innocent side to her. But tonight she was gonna be the beast that being with a nigga like me made her.

Larissa didn't go to the back part of the building the one time she was up here. So she didn't know where we were keeping that nigga. She turned back and looked at me with a questioning look and I pointed in the direction that was straight back past my office.

She continued on her way and stopped once she came to a door at the end of the hall. We kept that shit locked and beyond it was our spot that we handled mothafuckas. I hoped she was ready for what she was about to see because when it came to making niggas pay for the shit they did when they came against us, this shit was no joke.

I took out my key and unlocked the door. Draco and Silk followed behind me and once we were all inside I turned back around and locked the door. We always took safety precautions. The sight we walked in on wasn't too bad but that was all about to change.

My pits were surrounding Fe while he was laying in the center of the floor cradled into a fucking ball. My dogs were nothing to be fucked with. They would kill on my command only. I didn't want this nigga hurt until he saw the shit I had ready to show his ass.

Fe fucked up when he raped Larissa and let Carina's sick ass video tape that shit. I walked over to where he was at and told my dogs to heel. They sat down but still were growling at the nigga. They knew I wanted him dead, they could sense that shit.

As I approached he looked somewhat relieved but he shouldn't have. He should have been more scared of me than them damn dogs. I knelt low and pulled out one of my burner cells. I had been waiting to show this nigga this shit.

After I got LaLa back home safe and sound I sent a small team down to Belize. Usually I wasn't with touching families and shit, but the nigga in front of me violated in the worst way. After watching what the fuck this nigga did to Larissa I was determined to make him feel the same damn way before he left this earth.

The niggas I sent down had orders to find his wife and torture her. I thought about putting an order in to have her raped like Fe did to Larissa, but I wasn't the type of nigga to do no shit like that. There was some lines I wasn't willing to cross and that was one of the few.

In this game it was tit for tat and feelings about doing heartless shit had to be put out the fucking window. It was kill or be killed out here. As much as I hated hurting women, he should have never came after mine. That put everything on the damn table for me.

The nigga tried to close his eyes and stop from watching the shit. So I told Draco to come where I was at. He held Fe's head up by his forehead and neck.

"Watch that shit nigga. See how she begging them to stop?

"Fuck you! He said in his deep Belizean accent.

"How that shit feel?" I said in a voice that was ice cold.

After the video was done playing the nigga looked defeated. There was nothing worse than being helpless to the shit your loved one went through because of your choices. I knew exactly how his ass felt. But this shit that happened with my family was the last time I was gonna be put in that position.

It was time I adjust my plans for the future to ensure their safety since it seemed like no matter how much I upped security mothafuckas still were able to fuck with them. I wasn't willing to risk their lives anymore. I just needed to finish this shit out with Emeri and then some real changes were coming.

Larissa had been standing back and hadn't approached where we were at yet. She was hanging back letting me run shit. But once I put the phone back away she came forward. She gave me a look that let me know she was ready to murder this nigga. It was the same look that I'm sure was on my face.

She didn't ask questions about what was on the phone and what I was talking about when I asked Fe that shit. I was glad for that. I still hadn't told her I witnessed that shit and didn't plan on it. It was better to forget about everything altogether and put that shit behind us. It was time to look forward to better days and our future.

When Larissa came up to Fe she stopped within inches in front of him. I backed away. Draco was still standing behind him but had let his head drop back down.

"Stand his ass up." She commanded.

Draco pulled Fe up so that he was standing on his feet now coming face to face with LaLa. He may have been taller than her but she was staring his ass down like the no shit ass nigga he was.

She spit in his face and punched him in the eye. Not a weak ass punch either it was a closed fist hit that made a hard impact and caused his head to move back from it. LaLa really had them hands and could fuck a nigga or a bitch up if she was pushed to a certain point. This nigga had taken something away from her and he needed to pay for it.

The punch was only the beginning for Fe. LaLa continued to rain down blows on him and then kneed him in the balls. After that he tried to slump over but Draco held him up from behind while holding onto his hands that were tied behind his back.

Larissa didn't seem anywhere near satisfied when she let up. Her chest was heaving up and down from the work she was putting in but that shit didn't seem to phase her either. She turned to the left and spotted the table over against the far wall that had our tools for torturing mothafuckas. She started walking over to that shit and I went right along with her.

She let her hand brush against the top of each one as if she was trying to find the worst shit possible to handle this nigga. Finally, her hand rested on a sludge hammer. She picked the hammer up and checked it out.

Then grabbed a smaller hide knife. That shit was for skinning animals but came in handy when trying to get niggas to talk. There was no limit to the shit you could get somebody to tell you if you applied the right kind of pain and pressure.

LaLa was on the revenge shit though and until that was satisfied she was gonna continue to put in work. When she was finished Fe would be dead.

As she turned to walk back over to Fe our eyes met and I saw the look of sadness and anger behind her actions. She was hurt and even though this was something that she needed to do, it was hard on her. I couldn't fully understand what she was feeling, but I knew how watching what the nigga did to her made me feel. I reached out and grabbed her upper arm and pulled her in for a deep ass kiss.

"Ya'll some sick ass mothafuckas. Wait til this nigga handled first!" Draco's stupid ass yelled out with a tone of sarcasm before Silk joined in with laughter lightening the intense mood and moment that passed between us. Those were my niggas though.

"Fuck you. Let my wife handle shit how she see fit. Go take care of business bae." I said right back to both their asses.

LaLa turned back around and I smacked her hard on the ass before she continued on her way over to where Draco was still holding Fe. Before she made it all the way over I flipped both those hating ass niggas off.

Larissa got right back to work and slipped the knife in her back pocket. She picked the sludge hammer up and brought it down in a hard ass swinging motion slamming that shit into one of Fe's knee caps. His leg buckled under the impact and you could hear the bones crack from the shit. She didn't pause before she did the same thing to the other knee once Draco pulled him back up. He basically had to hold him up because his legs couldn't hold any weight.

After the second knee was fucked up he dropped to the ground and LaLa told Draco to let him stay there. She stood over top of him and brought down one last blow with the sludge hammer down on his dick. Draco and Silk both turned away when that shit happened. But they hadn't seen what the nigga did to my wife. I watched every fucking thing. Larissa bent down low like I did when I showed him the video of his wife being tortured.

She pulled out the knife and used her free hand to grab ahold of his chin. She squeezed that shit hard as hell while she spoke the last words he would ever hear.

"You thought you were gonna win nigga. But I'm gonna be the last face you see before you die." She said.

After the words left LaLa's mouth she leaned forward more while she was still squatted down between the nigga's legs. She pressed the knife into the flesh of Fe's neck on one side. Then she pushed down and dragged the knife across his neck slitting that shit deep as fuck.

Blood seeped out and completely covered Larissa's hands. She brought the knife back and watched Fe gurgle and lose consciousness in pain. She still didn't get up even after it was clear he was dead.

I walked over to her and grabbed her by the shoulders lifting her up and bringing her into my body while I turned her around. She dropped the knife and it clanked on the cement floor. LaLa was crying a silent body shaking cry and I rubbed her back. I didn't say shit but instead lifted her up and cradled her in my arms before walking towards the door that led to the front part of the warehouse where my office and shower were.

After unlocking the door and closing it behind me, LaLa buried her face into my chest while I continued to carry her into my office. Once inside I went ahead and walked right into my bathroom that was attached. Everything was state of the art and the lights came on when someone entered from the motion detector. I placed both her feet on the floor and went to turn on the shower.

She was still standing there crying and trembling. I knew that her reaction to killing that fuck nigga was more to do with what she experienced at his hands than actually committing the act of murder itself. This wasn't her first body, but it was the first time she was confronted with the shit she went through since being held hostage.

While the shower was heating up I went ahead and got undressed. Then I started taking off Larissa's clothes one piece at a time. I lifted her shirt up over her head and then unsnapped her bra. Her big ass titties sat up perfect like always. Out of instinct, I reached out and grabbed both of the mothafuckas rubbing on her nipples until they were hard.

Larissa was my heart and her hurting, was hurting me. I was gonna make her feel better and then once we came out of the shower it would really be a new beginning for us. We were gonna wash away all the shit that had happened as a result of me being in the streets. I was gonna make sure she never went through no shit like this again. She deserved better.

I unzipped her pants and pulled them off too. I was tempted to spread her pussy wide and start sucking on the fat mothafucka before we even made it in the shower. But decided against it.

I opened the shower door and LaLa stepped inside while I followed right behind her. My dick was hard as fuck and had been that way since I first watched her walk in the building. Shit it had been hard since before I even proposed. Seeing the big ass rock on her finger did something to me too.

The shower was almost the same size as the one at our house making the shit I was about to do to Larissa possible. When I was done with her ass the only thing that was gonna be on her mind would be the fucking we did.

I went ahead and picked up the soap and lathered up the wash rag. I took my time washing Larissa"s back and the rest of her beautiful body. Making sure to let the water wash away all the blood that was covering her hands and face.

Once the water ran clear, I grabbed the shampoo and massaged that shit through her hair. Her hair was sexy as fuck and I loved playing in it. Every part of Larissa was fucking perfect.

I got LaLa completely cleaned but I wasn't done with her yet. I was determined to make her forget all the shit of the last few hours of us being here.

I pulled Larissa back into me and let her feel my hard dick that sat just above her ass. She knew what time it was. I gripped her ass and kissed and sucked my way down her back with my mouth, getting down so that her ass was in my face. I spread her shit wide like I wanted to do earlier and pushed one of her legs up onto the ledge. I started eating her pussy from the back and of course she tried running from my tongue game.

I didn't let her go no fucking where. Instead I held her tighter and moved one of my hands around her and cupped her pussy hard as hell. That shit had her bucking back against my mouth.

I started vibrating my tongue and then flicked it in and out of her pussy. Once I let up and brought my tongue up along the crack of her ass that shit sent her over the edge. While she was cumming I rubbed her clit hard and fast making her have an even bigger orgasm.

Larissa's legs were weak as fuck after the shit I did to her so I stood up so I could support her better. My shower's marble tile gave us better traction. So I lifted her up and leaned her up against the side shower wall. Her back was up against that shit and her legs wrapped around me. My dick was sitting just below her pussy. But before I gave her the dick, I wanted to make sure she was straight.

"I'm sorry La for everything I let happen to you. I'm done with this shit ma. I'm not putting you in harm's way no fuckin' more. After this last move you ain't gotta worry 'bout shit no more." I said trying to ease her mind.

I wanted to let her know that there would be no next time for shit like this to go down. I was tired of losing when it came to my family. I started out hustling with only one thing being important to me and that was making money.

Once I met Larissa shit changed for me. Getting paper wasn't an issue anymore. I had so much bread stacked it didn't make any sense. Now I needed to do whatever it took to protect what was mine. I was ready to get out before it cost me more than it already had.

"I love you Messiah." She said before kissing me. Then she pulled back and rested her head against the shower wall and said, "Now fuck me and make me forget all the bad shit. Make it go away."

She said that shit in a sexy ass voice and I was gonna do just that. I stuck the big monster in after she said that shit and of course her ass screamed out and tried to back up, but there was nowhere for her to go. She was stuck taking the mothafucka.

I used my hands to support her while I gripped her ass cheeks again and started moving in and out of her digging deep in them guts. I picked up the pace and fucked her harder. She sunk her nails deep into my shoulders which let me know I was hitting it right.

Her titties were bouncing and rubbing up and down on my chest. I leaned down and sucked on them while I kept the same rhythm. She moved her hands onto my head in my dreads that were tied up. She always loved to play with them while I fucked her.

I slowed down and gave her some slow deep strokes.

"Just like that ma. Don't fuckin' move." I said.

Larissa was tightening her pussy muscles and her walls clenched down on my dick causing my nut to rise. She was on the verge of cumming right with my ass. Me telling her to stay still had the opposite affect on her. That shit `made her go harder.

I wasn't ready to bust yet, so I pulled out and backed up to let her down on the shower floor. LaLa was spoiled behind my dick game but her ass knew I liked to be in charge and wasn't about to let her run shit. She stared at me and then got this sexy ass smirk on her face before she dropped down.

She looked up at me with her hand gripping my hard dick.

"What you want me to do then?" She asked looking sexy as fuck.

I loved when she played the obedient role and let me be in control.

"Bless me with that mouth girl." She knew exactly what she was doing too.

She continued to grip my dick with just the right amount of pressure while the water ran over us. Looking down at her handling my shit made me feel like a fucking king. She started moving her hand up and down my shaft faster and gave me one last look before she opened up and let my dick slide down her throat.

Even after the monster caused her to gag LaLa kept going. That shit just coated it with more spit making it extra sloppy. Then Larissa slowed down and started fucking around with just the tip of my dick, humming on the shit making her mouth vibrate. I was about to cum after a few minutes of her blessing me with her head game.

I wanted to bust in her fat pussy though.

"Get up and toot that ass up for daddy. Make that shit clap." I said meaning every fucking word.

She obeyed just like I knew she would and turned around and took a couple steps over to the back of the shower, leaned over and put her hands on the lower ledge for support. LaLa started making her fat ass clap and the water caused a loud ass slapping noise.

The sight of her bent over and twerking right in front of me doing exactly what I told her was some other level sex shit. She was the only woman who fit me in every way even fucking.

I stepped behind her and held her hips tight. I knew I was leaving a hand print on her hips but she loved that rough shit just like me.

I pulled her back into me and let my dick find the base of her pussy. Once I was all the way in I started fucking her again. All that could be heard was the sound of us fucking and LaLa's screams.

I didn't give a fuck if my niggas heard that shit or not. I was trying to erase any bad shit from her mind. My dick was gonna be the only thing she could think about afterwards from the way I was fucking her.

"Messiah, Fuck I'm 'bout to cum again." She let out between moans.

"No the fuck you not. Hold that shit in until I cum with you." I told her ass.

Her body started shaking and I felt her pussy quivering, so I knew she was trying to hold that shit in. I pushed down on her back with one of my hands causing her ass to come up even more. That was all she fucking wrote.

We both cummed after that and I stayed planted deep inside her for a minute while my legs recovered from going weak.

Her pussy was so good that whenever I busted in her my whole body was affected for a minute after. No other bitch's pussy did that shit to my ass.

The love I had for Larissa came through when we fucked. It was a mind and body experience. We were connected to each other in every way, except one. And that was in marriage. But after tomorrow that shit would be changed too.

We washed each other up after the sex we just had and by the time we were out and dressed all the bad shit was like a distant memory. I had to give Larissa some of my extra clothes I kept in my office and even with my shit on she was beautiful as fuck. Just like the first night she stayed over with my ass.

Even though so much shit had gone on between us and we had changed over the last couple years, the love was still stronger than ever. I was ready for tomorrow so she could officially be mine. Since I had been claiming that shit since the first time I saw her, it was only right to make it legal and binding.

Shanice

I was so excited for Larissa. She deserved to be happy after all the shit she had been through. I couldn't wait to get all the details about what Money did for the damn proposal. If it was anything like the other shit he did for her then it was gonna be nothing but the best. He was crazy behind my girl.

Larissa and Money got back from the surprise proposal later than I expected. I was anxious about the shit because I planned on meeting up with Deandre after I left from staying to watch the babies. I wanted to go ahead and get this face to face over with once and for all. I needed my ex to stop with all the messages and shit he kept doing.

If I met up with him on my way home and made it quick it would keep Silk from finding out. The only reason I was really even meeting up with the nigga was to keep him from fucking shit up for me and my relationship. I knew deep down that was Deandre's real intention and I was gonna put a stop to all his foolishness tonight.

Silk was my everything and I wasn't about to let Deandre come between us. Dre and Silk were complete opposites besides them both being attractive. Now I knew real love thanks to Silk. He always made sure I was taken care of and there was no limit to the lengths he would go to, to show me how much I meant to him. When I finally gave him a real chance it was the best decision I ever made. We were on the same page when it came to so much shit.

Even his daughter was now like my own. In the short amount of time since I was introduced to her, I already found myself missing her each time she had to go back to her stupid ass mama. That woman was the sorriest excuse for a mother. She kept pushing the baby on Silk more and more. Which was fine with me because I looked at her like my own.

I never understood how a mother could put themselves before their child. Really that bitch needed some sense beat into her and very time I spoke on the shit to Silk he acted like I was overreacting. That shit made me think he still had some unresolved feelings for the hoe. But no matter what I was gonna make sure Kiandra was good. She was the sweetest and cutest little girl and if her dumb ass mama didn't do right, I would pick up the slack.

Silk was hard core and heartless in the streets. But for some reason he had a soft spot for females. It was irritating as hell sometimes. In my opinion, if shit didn't involve his mama, me or Kiandra then there should be no place for my man's sentiment. I was stingy with my nigga's love and feelings.

After Larissa got back home and I was outside the house, I sent a text too Dre letting him know I would be at my parents' house in about fifteen minutes to meet up. I already talked to my mother and let her know I was gonna be by the house.

My parents were out of town this weekend so it worked out perfectly. Deandre used to come over all the time when we were together. It was fucked up that both my mother and father would rather me be with his dog ass than Silk.

They were always were fooled by the show Dre put on just like so many people that crossed paths with him. The difference was Silk wasn't fake about shit. He was exactly who the hell he was, and that was a straight out thug ass nigga. And I loved that shit.

Dre was the exact fucking opposite and was the definition of a low down snake who would do anything to get what he wanted. So when he first met my parents and I was only fifteen he said all the right things, dressed like a preppy ass boy and never let on that he was so much older than me.

At the time I felt like him doing all that shit to impress my family was his way of showing me how much he loved me. The truth was he was a hundred times worse than Silk in every way. He was the grimiest nigga I had ever met and as I got older I realized how much of a young naïve girl I was when I was with him.

I didn't blame myself though. I was just a kid after all and everything that I went through with him helped teach me the type of man I didn't want to fuck with and ultimately led me to being with Silk. So I wasn't mad about shit that was in the past.

The shit with Deandre had me nervous, not because I had any feelings for the nigga but because I had no fucking clue why he wouldn't leave me the hell alone. He wouldn't let up and wasn't budging with getting in contact with me. We hadn't spoken since the beginning of his bid when I made my last visit. That was two years ago so I was really wondering what the hell was gonna come out his mouth. If he thought he still had a chance with me then he was a bigger fool than I thought. But I had prepared myself to deal with this nigga and now I was just ready to get the shit over with.

I pulled into the driveway and stayed in my car for a minute to calm my nerves. Usually I would have smoked a blunt to keep my emotions in check, but with this nigga I needed to keep my head completely clear and my guard up.

I went ahead and got out the jeep and walked up to the front door. Using my key I let myself in and turned on the lights in the

151

hallway and then walked over to the kitchen and living room to turn on those switches too. Not even five minutes later the doorbell sounded and when I looked through the peephole Deandre was standing there like I figured he was.

I took a deep breath and unlocked the door trying to keep my composure. He pulled back the screen door and we stood there for a minute in an awkward silence. One thing that I couldn't complain about was how sexy Dre was. There was no question about that shit. That was why I was so weak for his ass in the first place. Whenever I was around him from the first time we met, my panties stayed wet I swear.

Seeing him now and being near him was not having the same affect it used to have on me. I could admit he was good looking. But to me all his fucked up ways overshadowed any appeal he used to have. I knew the real Deandre and he wasn't anyone I wanted anything to do with in the future whatsoever.

Once he stepped inside I turned around awkwardly and went over to the kitchen island and sat down in one of the stools. Deandre followed behind me but instead of sitting down in one of the other stools he went to the other side of the island and stood there with his hands on the counter top looking right into my eyes.

I guess he was trying to gauge my reaction to him or some shit. But he wouldn't find a thing. My feelings for the nigga standing in front of me were all the way gone and anything I was left with was all bad shit. I don't know what he expected to see reflected back at him from the look I was giving his ass.

He licked his lips and had to say some dumb shit like I knew he was gonna.

"I can't get no love Neesy?" He asked.

"You know damn well I didn't agree to meet up with you because I wanted to. So say the shit you came here to say. Since you can't take a damn hint." I said with all the nasty attitude I could muster.

"Yeah okay. You so mad at the one nigga who always loved you and had you're back, while you act like that nigga Silk can do no wrong." He shot back.

I stood up and pushed the stool in. It was obvious that Dre was here on some hating ass shit and really didn't have a damn thing to say to me that I needed to hear.

Just like I thought, this meeting was pointless. Then him talking out his neck about my man was something I definitely wasn't gonna sit back and listen to even if Silk wasn't here. It was time for Deandre to go. I just needed to make sure he got the fucking message that I didn't want shit else to do with his ass from here on out.

"Get the fuck out Dre. I agreed to this shit because you kept saying you needed to tell me some shit. I knew you were gonna be on some bullshit though because that's the type of nigga you are. So listen to me when I say this shit and listen good. Stay the fuck away from me! Whatever we had is way past over and I moved on." I basically yelled at his stupid ass.

Dre seemed unaffected by my yelling at him. He came around to where I was standing and stood close right in front of me.

"That nigga ain't shit either. Ask him what the fuck happened to Brian and then you'll know who really in your corner shorty." He said in a calm tone.

Then he leaned over and kissed me on the cheek before heading out the front door.

After he was gone I stayed at my parents' house for another hour or so trying to wrap my head around what had just happened. I was pissed off to the max and didn't know why. I didn't want shit to do with that nigga. But obviously if I needed to stay here and get myself together before going back home it was something.

I loved Silk with all my heart. Now that Deandre put doubt in my head I had to get rid of that before I went home to him. I was one to always speak my mind, so there was no telling what the fuck I was bound to say if I showed up feeling how I was when Deandre left.

While I was on my way home my thoughts kept going back to what Dre said. He mentioned my cousin Brian. Brian was my closest cousin growing up. He was the one who always looked out for me and made sure I could take care of myself when I was in the hood. Over the years he checked countless niggas for fucking with me or even trying to. Deandre made it sound like Silk was responsible for his disappearance.

If that was true I didn't know what I was gonna do. Brian was like a brother to me more than a cousin. He went missing last year and thinking about that shit always left a bad taste in my mouth to begin with. Brian wasn't a bitch and I knew for a fact he was working for Money.

With the small amount of shit I actually did know about that happened in Money's organization there was no telling what the fuck really went down with my cousin. I'm sure there was some shit that could have went left but I didn't wanna think the worst just because Deandre said some shit. He was the least trustworthy nigga alive.

At that time me and Silk weren't even together. We had been talking but it was after the first time we tried to meet up and that dumb stripper hoe came up on us popping off at the mouth. It wasn't until after Brian was gone that I really gave Silk a chance.

I mentioned Brian to Silk plenty of times, especially whenever I was recalling some childhood memory I had. So if he was involved in any way with some foul play when it came to my cousin it was gonna be fucked up in the very least. There was so many times when he could have said something to me. I was getting ahead of myself though. It was probably just some shit that my ex was filling my head with that had no truth to it. Deandre was on that hating shit and wanted me to doubt the man I loved.

I calmed myself back down before making it back home to the place I shared with Silk. While pulling in and parking I immediately noticed Silk's car wasn't parked in its usual spot. That meant he probably wasn't home. I breathed a sigh of relief.

At least I wouldn't have to lie to him more than I already did. He only went out at this time of night if it was some important shit. I wouldn't call and bother him but I did shoot him a quick text telling him I loved him.

Once I was inside I hurried my ass upstairs damn near running just in case he came home before I was settled in. The less it seemed like some shit was off the less chance of him being suspicious. Here I was acting like I fucked another nigga or some shit. But I felt like I betrayed our relationship by meeting with Dre. To be honest, I was keeping a lot of secrets from Silk and none of that was gonna sit right with him if he found out.

After taking a quick shower and moisturizing my body from head to toe I folded back the bed covers and got comfortable underneath. I loved our big ass bed. It was so comfortable with the Egyptian sheets and huge down comforter. I preferred to sleep naked, and was hoping that once Silk made it home he would wake me up to some good ass dick.

Tomorrow we were leaving around eight o'clock to catch a flight to Belize where Larissa and Money were getting married. It was gonna be a day to remember filled with family and love. What they shared was similar to what me and Silk had. It was some real life soulmate shit. I really loved my man and never got enough of him. With thoughts of Silk and his sexy ass body I finally fell into a comfortable sleep.

Larissa

It seemed like I didn't sleep a wink last night. After getting back from taking care of Fe once and for all, I broke down all the way. I was so grateful that Messiah helped me through that shit. I always worried that he saw me as weak.

In the life we lived I needed to be strong. Strong for Messiah and now my son. I really tried to live up to the expectations that were placed on me by my man and by myself, but what happened to me and my unborn at the hands of that man and Carina was something that changed me. The hurt and pain was now only bareable because I felt that I got my retribution.

Being with Messiah was already turning me into a boss. But in order to deal with the pain that I went though I had to turn cold and bitter to get through that shit during the experience and afterwards. I didn't want to be a person that held onto that. I wanted to be able to move forward and be the happy person I was before being taken by them.

Killing Fe was a relief for me. The two people who tormented me were no longer walking this earth and I felt like I would be able to become myself again. Maybe more wise to the world and definitely not the passive girl I once was. But I had more hope for my future.

There was no question that I was gonna spend the rest of my life with the love of my life, Messiah Lawson. Through the good and bad I was gonna stay by his side. I hoped that our future would hold more good and less of the bad that we had already been plagued with. But until the day I died my heart was his.

Today we were flying out to Belize to get married. When Messiah proposed to me last night I was completely caught off guard. Sure we planned to get married one day and we always talked about our future. Shit he was ready to make shit official a whole year ago when we were down in Miami. But I wasn't expecting it to happen yesterday, especially since it was our Son's birthday. I usually wasn't one for surprises but he did a good ass job with this one.

Messiah put a lot of thought into each of the presents he gave me yesterday too. He wasn't even a romantic nigga most the time. More of a "what you see is what you get" type of man. But when it came to me he always went out of his way to make me feel special. He remembered little shit which made the proposal more heartfelt.

I loved everything about his ass and as I thought about him a gigantic smile came to my face like it always did. It was the same smile I wore after he approached me the very first time in the parking lot where we met.

As I sat in my vanity chair brushing my hair out I thought about all the possibilities our future might hold. Messiah was still sleeping soundly behind me in the bed and was snoring. I know his ass was knocked out behind that pussy I put on him last night.

MJ walked into our room holding hands with Silk's little girl Kiandra. I swear he was his father's son acting like he ran shit and a damn ladies' man already. It was cute though. When he saw I was up he released Kiandra's hand and ran over to me.

"Mommy, daddy sleep." He said like he was mad or something.

"Why don't you wake him up?" I said back to my pride and joy.

I loved him more than anyone else alive even his daddy. I kissed him on the cheek and sat him back down on the ground. Of course he took off running towards our bed like I knew he would. He climbed up and made his way over to Messiah and started jumping up and down laughing. Messiah started moving in his sleep and finally woke all the way up. He snatched MJ up by grabbing him from his stomach and playfully tossed him down onto the bed next to him. MJ just started laughing harder and tried getting back up to start jumping again.

"Alright. You got me boy." He started tickling MJ on his stomach making him roll around.

By this time Kiandra figured it was safe to join in on the fun and she jumped up to play with MJ and Messiah. He was making them both roll with laughter. I sat back enjoying the sight in front of me. Messiah was the best father and provider for our family. He would take care of us by any means necessary. Most people didn't get a chance to see this side of him and I felt truly blessed each and every day that I was able to call him my own.

"Alright you two. We need to get ready so we can catch our flight. We're going on a trip." Messiah finally let up and told the kids.

"Where?" MJ"s little inquiring mind asked.

"I'm making your sexy ass mama my wife." He said back.

MJ was only one so he didn't understand all of what Messiah was saying. He was smart as hell for his age, but still a baby. So I went ahead and got both the kids and went to take them to MJ's room to get them ready. Kiandra had a bag with some of the cutest clothes. I could tell how much my best friend loved this little girl and was sure all of the stuff in the bag was things she bought for her. She just had a big ass heart like that.

The way she stepped up to the plate and played the step mother role made it seem like it wasn't so bad. Me and Messiah really hadn't talked about the possibility of him being a father to that bitch Che's baby, but with how big she was in New York I knew she must be close to her due date. Almost two months had passed since all that drama and chaos unfolded in our lives.

Like with every other difficult situation that was thrown at us, we not only survived making it through all the BS, but we came out on top of the shit stronger together than before. We went through some of the worst and most painful shit a person could and yet we were still together and loved each other more and more.

I was now confident that I would be able to stand by my man, my soon to be husband, if the child was in fact his. I understood that the baby was innocent to everything and whether I was his/her biological mother or not, the baby would still be a part of Messiah. I loved him so much that loving his child wouldn't be that hard. I really didn't' want to deal with any baby mama drama, but if I needed to I would check that bitch. I already knew Messiah would put her in her place though. He didn't do that disrespect shit period as he always said.

Thinking about our future together brought another smile to my face. He really surprised the hell out of me with the proposal last night and then the trip to Belize today was so damn over the top. That was him though. I finished getting the babies ready and brought them downstairs so we could leave and catch our flight on time.

When I made it down the stairs, Messiah was already waiting like usual on my ass. He was staring me down like he was ready to fuck. Shit he was always ready to fuck so I wasn't surprised. I set the kids down and wrapped my arms around his neck burying my head in the nape of his neck. I loved the way my nigga felt and smelled. I couldn't' get enough no matter how much I was around his ass.

Messiah reached both his arms around and palmed my ass that was sitting up nice in some stretch joggers. He cupped the bottom of each cheek and squeezed them while pulling me close. Of course his dick was hard as hell and was poking my damn stomach when he did that shit. I pulled back and looked down between us and then back up at him while tilting my head to the side. His cocky ass winked and licked his lips, before slapping me on the ass and backing up.

I took that as my cue to finish getting the kids' stuff and get them in the car. We needed to leave if we were gonna make it on time. Messiah usually would have tried to fuck but for some reason he was acting like we needed to get going. Maybe he was nervous about actually marrying my ass and being tied down. Whatever it was, it definitely was a different side to him.

We made it to the airport hangar on time and were left waiting on Silk, Shanice, Draco and my sister so we could leave. My brother Enzo and Messiah's brother Biz couldn't go with us. It was disappointing but nothing they could help.

Enzo was handing business that couldn't wait back in Chicago so I understood. Biz couldn't come with us because he was out on parole and couldn't' leave the country. In a few months Messiah would be able to pull some strings. But with him just getting out he was hot right now. The feds would be watching his ass close. So Messiah had to be smart about how he moved when it came to his brother.

Messiah's mother was already down in Belize apparently and had been since last night. She left right after MJ's part on a private flight so that she could make sure everything was in order for the ceremony later today.

It all felt surreal, like I couldn't believe I would be a married woman by the end of the day. It still hadn't hit me yet. While we waited for the rest of the group Messiah poured us two flutes of champagne. I usually hated champagne but he made it a mimosa and that shit was good as hell.

Draco and my sister Lorraine came in the plane not too long after we got there. Those two were hand in hand all lovey dovey and shit. My big sister was five years older than me. Draco was the same age as me and Messiah. I would have never seen him going after an older woman with his crazy ass. But maybe it was just the thing he needed to settle down. They really seemed to be into each other and he couldn't keep his hands off her even though they just met.

Seeing the people around me happy was everything. I wanted us all to have the best of the best. What I felt for Messiah was a feeling that I hoped everybody I surrounded myself with was lucky enough to experience in their life.

There was nothing like being at complete peace with your life and being able to fully live in the now with a joy that came from within. That was what Messiah and I were able to build over the course of our relationship. Everything wasn't always easy, shit it was far as hell from that. But we made it work and shit was working out for us and those around us.

Shanice and Silk came into the plane not long after and the entire good vibe that was previously in the air seemed to disappear with them. That was bizarre as hell because those two were usually the most solid couple there was. They rarely went through shit and the things that had come their way were small in my opinion.

My bestie definitely had a funky ass attitude towards him, so he must have done some dumb shit. It was usually on the niggas to fuck up somehow. I just hoped it didn't' have anything to do with Shanice's ex trying to come back in the picture.

Shanice was being extra and didn't even sit by Silk. Instead she made her way over to where I was sitting and sat on the other side of me. Messiah caught the meaning of her wanting to chill with me, so he gave me a look and winked at me before standing up and going over to where silk was at.

Not before he squeezed my thigh causing a jolt to run through my body from his touch. Making me hornier than I already was since before we left the house. It was like I was ready to pounce on his ass for real.

As I sat there lusting over my fiancé, Shanice started up a conversation.

"Can you believe that nigga didn't even come home 'til an hour ago?! Then he hasn't said shit to my ass either. I don't know what they fuck his problem is. But I'm not 'bout to feed into his ass. Fuck Silk." She said in a whisper so that I was the only person who could hear her.

I'm sure the others knew she was talking shit about his ass though because she was giving him a death stare the entire time she was speaking to me. There was more to it then she was letting on though. There was no way that Silk would be acting up like that for no reason.

He worshipped the damn ground Shanice walked on and always treated her like a queen. Not like a lot of men who claim they have a queen. He lived by that shit. To the point that he held doors open, let her walk in front of him, kissed her hand, all the extra shit even good men don't do. He did all that and more for her. She was cherished by that man.

So I had a feeling she did some foul shit. But I wasn't about to sit up here and judge her. I would always keep shit real with her because she was like my sister. But I would stand by her no matter what until the end of time.

"So there's no reason he's acting strange? Nothing happened last night after you left my house?" I asked her talking in a low voice to match hers.

She didn't answer. Instead she shook her head and then finally decided to tell me some shit that let me know she was fucked.

"I mean I met up with Deandre at my parents' house. But shit it was just to get him to leave me the fuck alone. But Silk don't know about it." She said the last part like a lightbulb just went off in her head.

She must have figured out that he knew. Our men were not just regular ass niggas in the streets. They were the fucking plug. Shit they were the plug to the plug. They were that damn big.

A lot of the time it was easy to forget the positions they held because the way they operated and how humble they were. It just didn't seem like they were as big and as dangerous as they really were. The truth was they could know whatever the hell they wanted to know. Touch whoever they wanted to.

That was why the shit that happened to me and our family was fucking with Messiah so bad. He really was the boss of half the country, and yet he wasn't untouchable and never would be. There were certain things though that our men always did know. One of those was where we were at. Especially in our hometown. Shanice should have known better.

Shanice was more knowledgeable about the street shit than me or at least she used to be. Now I was giving her ass a run for her money. She didn't even know about the two people I had murdered.

There was some things that I didn't speak on to anyone except Messiah. Mostly because he was there for both the murders that I committed. My reason for not telling her wasn't because I didn't trust her. It was because if the police ever questioned her I didn't want to make her an accessory to my crimes. I was protecting her.

She was beyond bold with meeting up with her ex. To make shit worse, she made it personal or at least that was what it was gonna seem like to Silk. Her parents didn't even wanna meet his ass, but she invited her ex over to their house. That was a low blow on her part.

No wonder he was acting salty towards her. She's lucky he didn't really show his ass. Because she deserved someone talking sense into her. Her ex was a no good ass nigga. He couldn't be trusted for nothing. Just meeting with him, even at her parents, was a risk. I don't know what the hell she was thinking.

"Girl you know who our niggas are right?" I asked more as a statement than a question.

"Fuck... I just wanted him to leave me alone. Nothing happened. But he tried to tell me Silk killed Brian's ass. I mean it makes sense. So shit I should be mad at his ass right now." Shanice told me.

"You two need to talk." Was all I said in response before I leaned back and reclined as much as possible in the seat.

I wanted to be by her side and would always have her back but until the two of them talked there wasn't much point in commiserating with her. In my opinion she was dead wrong for meeting up with that snake ass nigga in the first place.

I tried to warn her about this yesterday before the party and she didn't listen. I wasn't a told you so type of friend though. I'm glad that nothing more came of the situation then the two of them meeting up. I really didn't trust Deandre's ass for a minute and she put her safety at risk meeting up with him. Being with Silk meant she could be a target for niggas just like I was because of being with Messiah. She should have at least told Silk about him trying to contact her. She was on some shady shit. But right or wrong I would have her back.

"Yeah, yeah. But tell that nigga that." She grumbled back to me. I felt her recline next to me since my eyes were still closed.

I opened my eyes just a peek and saw her next to me closing her eyes too.

"Night, night bitch." I said with a smile on my face.

"I love you too girl. Yes honey we need to catch some shut eye because today is about to be lit. Congrats again bestie!" She said.

I was so glad to have a friend like her. I was reminded again that today really was the big day and within a matter of hours I would officially be Mrs. Lawson. It was like a dream come true.

Silk

I don't what the fuck Shanice was on. But I wasn't one for the games and the bullshit she was up to. I knew exactly where the fuck my woman was at, at all times. She must have lost her damn mind to be going behind my back meeting up with her ex. Shit I was outside her parents' house the whole time she was inside with that fuck nigga.

It took everything in me not to bust into the house and drag her outside and away from that bitch ass nigga. The only reason I didn't was because I wanted to give her the benefit of the doubt and give her an opportunity to come clean about the shit she was up to. I prayed she knew better than to cheat on me because that would be the end of everything for us. Even if she wasn't fucking around it was a betrayal of trust for her to be sneaking around doing shit behind my back.

Not to mention I didn't' trust no nigga around what was mine. To make it even worse I knew everything there was to know about her ex. The mothafucka was the worst type of nigga. He was a pathetic ass scammer and con artist. He wasn't really about shit other than using those around him to live off of. He wasn't even important enough to have a title like pimp or a stick-up nigga. He didn't have a hustle except to exploit bitches and his own family to make money.

I didn't have an ounce of respect for any nigga like him and definitely wasn't worried about his ass being in competition with me. But the fact remained that Shanice did that shit behind my back and even had the nigga over to her family home. What type of shit was that.

Her ex was exactly the type of nigga who would jump at the opportunity to use Shanice to come up now that he knew she was with me. She should have known that off of all the shit she told me about her past that involved him alone. As I sat on the plane half listening to my day one nigga talk about his plans for after the wedding as far as the take-over, I couldn't help to keep thinking about my own personal shit.

This was the worst time for my personal shit to cloud my judgment. Today was supposed to be all about my fucking brother taking a big ass step and tying the knot with Larissa who was like a sister to me too. I wanted to show my full support and celebrate as a family with everyone in attendance. Then tomorrow we were gonna execute the plan that we spent the last few months perfecting and finally take out Money's father. There was absolutely no room for a single fucking error.

I knew I was gonna have to get shit out in the open and talk to Shanice for real once we landed in Belize. I couldn't afford to have this shit hanging over me right now. She didn't even deserve for me to bring the shit up to her. She should be the one to come clean, but I doubted that was ever gonna happen. I loved her ass to death but she was childish about some shit.

Shanice always put up a tough act and whenever she was in the wrong she wouldn't admit shit. That was probably the only thing that rubbed me the wrong way with her. Otherwise she was my perfect queen. I put her up on a pedestal because she deserved nothing but the best.

I knew I wasn't trying to lose her. But she needed to realize once and for all who the fuck I was and that I wasn't some punk ass nigga about to let her run all over me. I wasn't gonna allow her to lie to me or to put herself in danger. She should be able to trust me enough with any and everything. If we were really gonna last there wasn't gonna be no more of this bullshit she pulled. I just hoped that when I had this conversation with her I stayed calm enough and didn't strangle her ass. Her mouth could be reckless as hell.

I focused back in on the conversation that Money and Draco were having. It was too early in the morning to start drinking. I wanted to keep my senses for the shit we were discussing and for when I talked to Shanice.

So I only accepted the blunt that Draco had in rotation for a minute, taking one pull and then passing the shit back.

"So the niggas on the inside good?" I asked referring to the team of mothafuckas Money already had working for him inside the family organization in Belize.

They were supposed to be on Money's side and ready to support him taking over. The plan was to go to the estate on a friendly familial type visit so as not to raise any red flags on Emeri's side. Then when the three of us were on the premises we were gonna get the nigga alone, away from his most loyal bodyguard and take him out. Money was smart as shit and had everything down to even the damn room where Emeri would be killed mapped out.

We were counting on an outside explosion to draw the guards away from Emeri. If they somehow caught wind of the shit we were up to or decided to stay with Emeri instead of checking on the decoy then we would have to move to plan B. Our alternative plan called for a lot more chance and bloodshed. None of us three were scary niggas in the least. We would all rather die standing than to be killed on our knees as the saying goes. Wasn't no bitch made nigga in our group period.

"It's all set up. I heard from the nigga yesterday. He's my cousin and says I got the backing of the family. They're not happy with how my father's been treating them and are ready to make a move." He answered.

"So what's stopping them from trying to take us out once he's gone? It all might be a set up for them niggas to take control of shit."

"I got that shit covered don't worry." Money said keeping the details under wraps.

I trusted my nigga a hundred percent. There was no other way to be out here in the streets. Most mothafuckas weren't to be trusted, but if you didn't have at least one or two loyal niggas by your side, you couldn't get far out here.

Draco and Money were my brothers and I would kill or take a bullet for them, just like I knew without a doubt they would do the same for me. Not that I was trying to die or anything. But shit happened.

Tomorrow would be just another day full of life and death consequences that came with the life we lived. Being boss ass niggas called for ruthlessness and risks sometimes. This is what we lived for.

Messiah (Money)

We landed in Belize a few hours after taking off. After everybody else exited the plane, I walked over to where Larissa was laid out in one of the reclining seats. I reserved a private jet for this trip so we were the only two passengers left. This may be the one I ended up buying after I took over my family's cartel down here since it was locally owned. I was gonna need some shit to get back and forth at the drop of a dime.

Larissa was beautiful as fuck. She looked good as hell even when she was sleeping. I leaned down and kissed her on the jaw then started sucking on her neck and shit. Her breathing picked up and her eyes fluttered open.

I knew her pussy was dripping wet ready for this monster dick. Knowing I was the reason for that shit always made me feel like a king. The pilot and stewardess were the only ones on board. I didn't' give a fuck about who was around. I would fuck LaLa without a second thought.

But I wasn't gonna give in until after we made shit official. This day was some real shit to me. I wasn't a soft nigga, but marriage mattered to me. There was no way I was about to give away my last name and make a vow before God to spend my life with any woman besides Larissa.

I never even thought I would ever consider getting married. But LaLa was mine and there wasn't a doubt in my mind she was the only one that I would ever want by my side. So I was gonna wait until after the ceremony and then I would break her pussy in. I was gonna be fucking my wife all night. I had never gone this long without fucking except after Larissa lost the baby. But it was a day worth doing things differently.

"We here La. Wake up ma." I said low.

"Why you playing with me Messiah?" She asked in a serious voice.

"You gotta wait to get this married dick." I said a little louder.

Then I slapped her on the thigh and stood all the way back up. She stretched her arms and then stood up wrapping her arms around me. Larissa was being all dramatic leaning her weight into me and pulling herself close as hell to me. I loved the way her body felt on mine. My dick was hard as shit. But I was sticking to my plan of not fucking with her until after she was my wife.

So I turned around and started walking with her still holding onto me from behind. She even moved one of her hands lower and gripped my hard dick through my pants.

"Whatever nigga." She grumbled in a pouty ass voice before standing all the way up and letting her arms unwrap from around me.

I turned to the side and kissed her on the cheek. Then held her hand for her to step down behind me from the plane.

Belize was a damn paradise. Even though I didn't feel a connection to the place like I would have if I grew up knowing half my family came from here, I still thought of this as my second home. After the take-over Belize would be run by me so the shit only made sense. I didn't like a lot of shit about my father, but I respected the shit he built here. It was just time for the nigga to be replaced. I didn't have personal feelings behind the shit. It was just business.

The time I spent here was always a mission to me and about business nothing more. I already had a fucking family before his ass decided to come along. I didn't owe his ass shit. If he thought by coming to my rescue that ensured my loyalty then that was his downfall.

Loyalty was earned over time. I looked at it like I would have come out of the the shit Fe and Torio did without his ass anyway. If it had been my time to die, then I was fine with that shit too. I would never owe another nigga shit in this life. I stood on all ten by my damn self.

My brothers and niggas were the only partnas that I was loyal to. That shit wasn't based on blood but through time spent on the front lines. I would go to war for any of my niggas and they would do the same for me. That was why they were ready to make shit happen tomorrow.

We lived knowing that tomorrow wasn't promised and whenever we needed to bust guns there was never hesitation. This was the shit we chose and lived by. That was our mindset day in and day out.

I looked around and took in the beautiful ocean view and Larissa's reaction to the place. She seemed to be excited as hell and that let me know I was doing my damn job. I turned back around and tipped the flight staff, then started walking behind Larissa who already caught up with Shanice and her sister. Today was all about her so I was glad that she had those two her with her to share this day with.

There was a couple of Emeri's whips waiting on us. As far as he was concerned this was a family event and there wasn't shit for him to be worried about. That was another reason I wanted to get married down here. It was the perfect opportunity to surprise his ass when he least expected it.

My mama came down yesterday and finalized all the wedding plans that she had been helping me with over the last month. I was pulling out all the stops with this shit.

There wouldn't be no other marriages for me. This shit was once in a lifetime.

We weren't staying at the family estate because I wanted my wife and kids away from there for when shit popped off tomorrow. They would be out of harm's way already on their way back to the states before I made my first move. Larissa was involved in a lot of my shit now and I confided in her about everything except this.

I didn't want her involved with this shit at all. It was the biggest move I had ever made and there was no way, no matter how much she proved herself to be a beast in the streets, that I was letting her in on the shit. It was too dangerous and that's all there was to it.

I knew she wasn't gonna like the shit once she found out. But I could live with that. I couldn't live with myself if even one more fucking thing happened to her. She had been through too much. On God nothing was gonna hurt her or cause her pain again.

My family's safety was now my main motivation for making this move and it was the final move I would be making. After the take-over I was gonna step back and only play the role of supplier. Nothing more and nothing less. There would be no more hands on shit. It was time to put my family first, even before making money. I would still be stacking paper like never before. But the way I moved would be different.

I was gonna operate from remote locations and be a nameless connect. I wanted Silk and Draco to really run shit with the other bosses that we added to step up. I wasn't even gonna sit in on meetings or no shit. The only thing I would be doing was paperwork with no one even knowing it was me signing checks and shit besides my partnas.

Me and Larissas went ahead and said our goodbyes at the cars. We were making our own traditions with this shit. We stayed together the night before the wedding, but now there was only a few hours until we said our "I do's" and we needed to part ways and get ready.

Her and her girls were gonna be pampered and shit. It was all set up at the hotel we were staying at. We were gonna be married on the beach in front of the palce. It was gonna be a small ceremony with only close family and friends. I was mad that I even had to invite Emeri. But there wasn't shit to be done about it. If I didn't then he might think some funny shit was up.

Me and my niggas hopped in the Rafe that was waiting for us. This was actually one of the cars I purchased while I was down here. All the top of the line shit like these rides had to be imported. That was the type of money we were getting after the deal with my family cartel. I went ahead and took the driver seat. After staying down here for almost a fucking year I knew my way around. There was a lot of shit I was into while I was here.

But during the time no matter what shit I did to forget about Larissa and no matter how many bitches I fucked while down here, none of them came close to her. They couldn't even compete with LaLa on her worst day.

I drove through the streets like I owned the place. After tomorrow I would be running shit. Most of the mothafuckas down here knew who the fuck I was since I already made a name for myself while I was down here. But after the takeover they would never know I was the head of it all even after Emeri was gone.

I wasn't nervous about a damn thing. Not the shit with Emeri or getting married. There were about three hours until our wedding ceremony and I wanted to get right over to the hotel. That way I could kick back with my niggas and relax. The last thing I wanted was to get caught up out here with some bullshit before the wedding. There was nothing that was gonna stop this shit from moving forward.

After about twenty minutes we pulled into the hotel parking lot and I let the valet park the car. Me, Silk and Draco walked in like the boss ass niggas we were. All of us were dressed casual in our street shit. There was no reason to try and dress up and impress mothafuckas. They could think whatever the fuck they wanted about us. We were paid niggas. But we were always ready for whatever too.

I checked in and got the keys for all our rooms. I booked out the entire top floor for this shit. Then I had our luggage taken up while I made my way over to the lounge where my niggas were at. They didn't waste any fucking time ordering us a round of shots.

I sat down in one of the barstools so I could have a drink before heading up to the room to get ready and shit. I threw back the double shot of Hennessey that the bar tender sat in front of me. It was the only drink I was gonna have. I wanted to be a level headed when I recited my vows to LaLa.

All three of us sat around talking about the game that was on commercial. There was nothing like being able to sit back and relax with my niggas. Of course Silk and Draco tried to clown my ass for being the first to tie the knot.

I bet they wouldn't be too far behind my ass getting married either. They were as real and thorough as I was. When you're real ass niggas like us, there was nothing like finding a real woman to hold you down. Shit Silk was basically already married as it was. Even through Draco was wild as hell it seemed like he was really feeling Larissa's sister.

Silk ordered another round but I turned that shit down. His ass went ahead and downed his and mine for the hell of it. I could tell some shit was off between him and ol' girl. But we never got involved in each other's shit and I wasn't about to start. If he wanted to bring the shit up then that was one thing.

I just shook my head at his ass. I told him he better not be falling over standing next to me, or I would have to beat his ass for fuckin' up my wedding. We both laughed, but I was serious as hell. I would kick his ass if he fucked shit up.

"Whatever nigga, you know you can't bang with me. Don't think I'm a take it easy on your ass either 'cus it's your wedding. Come at me and see what happen." He said with a wide ass grin on his face.

There were plenty of times coming up that me, Draco or Silk went toe to toe with each other. It was nothing but love between us though. But we all had our own type of tempers. Sometimes swinging shit out was the best option. There wasn't no way we would be squeezing at each other though.

He knew that when we were younger I always came out the winner. Before I got a chance to call him on his shit, I felt a tap on my shoulder.

I turned around with my hand on my hip. No matter where the fuck I was or what the event I stayed strapped. I would not be caught slipping no matter how much security I paid for. There was nothing like being your own damn security.

My hand relaxed once I saw it was just Che. But my mood automatically was fucked up. I wasn't gonna let shit fuck this day up. Now this bitch was here with a sneaky ass look on her face. I knew instantly that she was up to some shady shit just like she was up in New York.

It had been a few months since she showed up claiming I was her baby's father. Now it was evident that she already gave birth and she already lost most of her baby weight. I didn't feel no type of attraction to her at all. She wasn't shit to me, never had been.

The situation she was trying to put me in didn't help either. Last time I saw her ass she tried to tell me she trapped me by poking holes in the condom. The more I thought about that shit the more off it seemed too. I still couldn't figure out why the hell this bitch was so intent on fucking with my life. What we had was never that serious. There weren't any feelings involved on my end whatsoever. We didn't even spend time together outside of fucking.

I remember most the times we fucked that I was the one who supplied the condoms. She never had access to my shit, so I was still real fucking skeptical that the baby was mine even before I saw him or her. No matter what though, this bitch needed to get the fuck on before LaLa saw her or word got back to her. If either her sister or Shanice caught wind of her being here they would without a doubt tell her. That was just how they rolled, just like me and my niggas.

But apparently she was on a mission or had a death wish because she tried talking to me.

"When you gonna see your daughter?" She asked in her thick accent that I was used to.

"Get the fuck on with your bullshit. I told you what it was. I'll set the test up when I touch back down in the States. For now stay the fuck away from me. This the last time I'm gonna tell you that shit." I said with finality.

Shit I was tired of the same shit with her ass. I was a real ass nigga. So I was gonna get a DNA test done now that I knew she had the baby. I would go from there. I wasn't gonna sit here and be worried about this bitch or the possibility of the baby being mine. Today was my fuckin' wedding day and I wasn't gonna let this shit ruin it period.

"But..." she said in a loud ass voice like she was trying to cause a damn scene.

I reached for my pistol again and had my hand on my hip when both Silk and Draco stood up and grabbed ahold of the bitch by the arms. They escorted her right on out of the bar area and then came back within a couple minutes.

They never got involved in my shit or checked a bitch on my behalf. I really wasn't playing with the hoe today, so I was glad for them taking care of the shit. My temper was one where I would shoot first without worrying about the consequences. Normally that wouldn't mean shit, but today I was trying to get married and shit.

I realized that she wasn't going nowhere though. After this trip I was definitely gonna make it a priority to get shit settled once and for all. I didn't like nothing or no one trying to hang shit over my head. Silk and Draco came back and both of them were cheesing like the whole ordeal was funny or something. Draco's ass was the first to speak on the shit.

"Man, you bout to pull your piece in here and kill a bitch. You trying to get married or not nigga?" He said laughing and shaking his head like he really said some funny shit.

"Had his hand on his shit and everything." Silk chimed in on the joke they were having between themselves at my expense.

"Fuck that bitch. You know how I get. Good looking out though." I said before grabbing the last one of Silk's shots that was still on the bar and throwing it back.

When I was ready to set a nigga or a bitch straight I was on mothafuckin' ten and now I needed to get myself calmed down before I went back upstairs. After gulping that shit down I stood up next to my niggas and adjusted my jeans and shirt.

"I guess it's time." I said before we started on our way out of the bar area.

It was really time for me to get ready and dressed for my damn wedding. This shit was finally happening and I couldn't wait to get it over with. Not only because I was more than ready to get my dick wet since it had been the longest I had gone without some of my damn pussy in a minute. But because this was the real fucking deal.

Larissa was gonna be my damn wife. With her by my side shit didn't get any better. She had been mine since day one, and now two years later that shit was gonna be on the damn record. My family would be complete after this shit.

If anybody would have tried to tell me this would be my life two years ago I would have laughed at them like they were the

189

craziest mothafucka alive. Larissa came into my life and changed every fucking thing for the better. I was ready for this shit.

Larissa

I swore to myself that I wasn't gonna cry during my wedding ceremony but standing at the end of the sandy isle that shit was proving harder than I thought. Everything was perfect.

The sun was beginning to set filling the sky with beautiful colors. The few rows of chairs were filled with our closest friends which were family to us and the rest with our small families. Messiah was standing there looking straight into my eyes with a serious look on his face. It was like he was speaking to my soul and the connection that always existed between us was stronger than ever in this moment.

I held back the tears that were threatening to fall from my eyes and started walking down the aisle to the sound of a piano playing in the background KC and JoJo's "All My Life" with a hired singer singing the lyrics. The song was perfect for the two of us. I didn't know how Messiah pulled all this off without me knowing anything about it. But he went all the way out and planned this to the T.

I didn't even choose my dress. Apparently he picked it out to suit my taste. It was a tight fitting lace top with two thigh high slits on either side. It was absolutely perfect and the stylist he had come do my hair and makeup was flown in from New York. He really was not playing around with this day.

I stood next to him in a trance just like always. It was like we were the only two around even though that wasn't the case. He was looking sexy as hell. His dreads were pulled back at the nape of his neck. He was wearing an all-white suit and looked every bit the boss that he was.

He was perfect. Messiah held his hands clasped in front of him still staring into my eyes. He let his eyes fall from the hold they had on mine and wander up and down my body. This nigga had absolutely no shame. He licked his juicy lips and then leaned forward kissing me deep and grabbing my ass while he pulled me close.

Our family and friends weren't no help either. They knew exactly how his ass was too. So they were clapping and hollering and shit encouraging his ass. The officiant, cleared his throat I guess to get our attention and finally when Messiah felt like it, he released his hold on me. Not before he whispered in my ear some nasty shit.

"You lucky this time ma. You not getting no dick 'til this shit over and you're mine for good." He said softly.

I got chill bumps from his breath on my neck and his sexy ass cologne turned me on even more. I was eager more than ever to say our I do's and get some dick. Call me what you want, but this nigga really did something to me every time I was around his ass.

I was pulled back to the present and the ceremony when the officiant began reciting the customary nuptials. It was a quick service and as soon as we said our vows it seemed like it was over. The entire thing was a surreal moment for me.

I would have never thought that this would be my life. That I would be a mother and wife all while pursuing my dreams. Thinking back on how shit played out it was amazing considering everything that me and Messiah had gone through together.

He was everything to me and we were exactly what the other needed when we each weren't looking for love to begin with. It was corny, but he was my other half. Everything I lacked he made up for and vice versa. We completed each other and built each other up into the people we were today.

I had absolutely no clue where we would be six months, a year, or five years down the road if we were still blessed to be alive on this earth. But I knew without a doubt that we would be together through it all no matter what. Us being together was some fate shit.

After the ceremony we went out on a yacht to have a sort of reception or more of an after party. We were involved with some street niggas and bosses at that so the way we lived and things we liked weren't suited for every place. It was nice to be able to unwind, drink and dance without worrying about some shit popping off too. Especially since we were in a foreign country.

Messiah reassured me that his family owned the fucking place as he always said. But I caught the undertone in that shit too. He wasn't feeling the family shit with his people down here. He made comments about his father being nothing to him. Plus I knew my man better than that. He was probably plotting some shit right now and that worried me because his father was the reason why a whole lot of shit came our way.

Thinking about his status and how Torio, Fe and even Carina all were connected to Messiah's father made me uneasy. He was the reason for them coming at us all out of retaliation.

In a way Emeri was the sole person responsible for everything being set in motion. Now that bitch Che was even connected to this shit. Being that she was from Belize and hooked up with Messiah while he was down here separated from me was just another situation that we had to face because of his family.

So it all gave me a bad feeling. I wasn't gonna speak on it to Messiah. He made a decision a while back to include me in the business and street shit that he was involved with. So I figured if he was really planning something he would let me know when I needed to know. It was crazy to think how far we had come and how much I had changed since getting with Messiah. Gone was the innocent and naïve young girl I was such a short while ago.

I realized that sometimes Messiah seemed to regret being the cause of so much pain and change in me. But this was the life I chose just like him. I was more than at peace with all of my choices, and if needed I would always step up and be the woman he needed by his side. There was nothing I wouldn't do to protect mine.

I was sitting in Messiah's lap sharing a blunt with him while Shanice and Silk were off on the top part of the boat. They had been acting funny towards each other the entire trip so far, but as the night went on they started gravitating more towards each other. Some shit was inevitable. I bet anything they would be back on good terms by the morning and after some fucking.

Draco and my sister were sitting across from us on the other side of the table. We were out on the main deck sitting at a big ass marble topped table. This yacht was top of the line just like everything in our lives at this point.

Messiah came up so much over the last couple years too and it seemed like he was meant for this lifestyle. It just fit him well. I still wasn't as comfortable with the shit as he was since I never envisioned my life turning out this way. But I was more comfortable with it then I used to be that was for sure.

We were all vibing out listening to the music that was blasting. I was staring up at the night sky admiring the stars that were shining down at us. Scenery like this made you feel closer to God and I said a quick thanks for allowing me to have the man of my dreams with me in this moment. I was high as fuck and gone a little bit off the few drinks I had had with my sister and Shanice earlier.

Messiah began gripping my thighs harder where the two slits were while I was comfortable in his lap. I already knew what that shit meant. He was done celebrating and ready to fuck. I guess we wouldn't be waiting until we made it back to our suite. I was down for whatever my husband wanted to do.

He gave Draco a head nod and held my hips easing me up off of him to a standing position. He slapped me hard on my ass sending a shock through my body but making my pussy wet with anticipation. My sister said goodnight and then went back to being cuddled up with Draco.

I started walking down towards the lower level that was indoors the cabin. Messiah put his arm around my waist and placed his hand on my pussy from behind. He applied exactly the right amount of pressure, he knew exactly what the fuck he was doing and he stopped me instantly in my tracks. He moved his hand from my pussy to the small of my back and steered me in the direction I guess he wanted me to go in instead.

After walking all the way over to the back of the boat. I braced myself by holding the railing tightly. The yacht wasn't moving much, we were rocking more or less to the smooth motion of the waves but my ass was still gonna hold on to this railing. I wasn't about to be overboard out here with these damn sharks. Not matter how fucked up I was, I wasn't' that messed up.

Messiah turned me around and then got down on his knees in front of me. My ass was against the railing now and thankfully it was high enough to brace most of my weight and sturdy enough because he lifted all of my skirt up and exposed not only my legs and thighs but my pussy as well.

The moon and stars shined down on us illuminating the deck so the shit was even doing something to me more. Of course I was prepared and didn't have shit on underneath leaving my pussy bare and exposed ready for Messiah.

He leaned in and used both of this hands to pull me by the ass into his face. I leaned my back up all the way into the high railing that met me just above the waist. Messiah let my legs fall over either side of his shoulders resting on them so that I was in the damn air.

His tongue entered my pussy first then he pulled it out and latched onto my clit. Somehow that nigga moved one of his hands enough to slide two fingers into me while not letting up on the sucking he was doing.

My body instinctively began grinding his face and I rode that shit out. I grabbed ahold of his dreads that had now come lose and let the feeling he was giving me overcome me all the way. My moans got louder and then he pulled away.

"Let that shit go LaLa and keep your fuckin' eyes open girl." He said loud as hell.

He really didn't give a fuck that other people where around and could catch us at any time. I didn't have a moment to think about that shit though because he began flicking his tongue back and forth fast as hell over my clit. I looked down at him like he told my ass to do, and like I knew he loved for me to do and then went back to moving my body to the rhythm.

My pussy tightened up and then he bit down gently on my clit with his fingers fucking me. My cum that was built up from not fucking for the last day gushed out. Messiah did like he always did and I swear drank up every drop. Finishing up he placed kissed on my pussy like he was tongue kissing my mouth instead.

He stood up and usually would have just started fucking me for real. But I took the opportunity to drop down to my knees and bless him with some bomb ass head. He was my husband now and I wanted to please him the same way he lived to please me.

I went ahead and unbuckled his pants and slid them down then did the same with his boxers. Of course his dark eyes were trained right on me watching me work. I smiled up at him and licked his big ass dick from the tip down to the base, letting my spit drip down to wet it up making it nice and nasty.

I used one of my hands to massage his balls and then moved my mouth down to pay them some attention. I started getting more creative with sucking Messiah's dick after the first few times. He loved all the nasty shit and the fact that I loved sucking his dick made him putty in my hands. I considered his dick mine and I loved it. It was sexy to me, just like every part of my man.

After licking his balls I moved back to the monster and let it slide as far as it could go down my throat causing me to gag some. There was no way around it, he was just that big that no matter how good my gag reflex was it was still gonna choke me.

He put his hand on the back of my head and applied some pressure letting me know he was done with me playing around. I got the massage and began moving my head up and down faster using my tongue to circle around the tip and flick back and forth at the base.

"Shit". I heard him say and knew he was about to bust with the way his body tensed up.

I continued to suck even harder creating more of a suction. You could hear the shit and I loved the effect I was having on him. My pussy was soaking wet again from sucking Messiah's dick. The shit had turned me on so much.

He started really fucking my mouth going harder and deeper causing tears to come to my eyes from being half choked. But still I kept sucking the life out of him until he released and his cum shot out. I swallowed every bit and kept sucking while I felt the last pulses from his orgasm. Then I stood back up to my feet.

Messiah lifted me up over his shoulder and carried me over to the cabin where I initially thought we were gonna go to make love. I was glad that he picked me up, because from the intense exchange between us and him making me cum from eating my pussy my legs were still weak.

After we made it inside and into the small bedroom down below. Messiah closed the door and turned on some music. I didn't even pay attention to what song was playing because I was so ready to feel my husband inside of me. Messiah went ahead and got naked with me eyeing every inch of his body. I was stuck like I couldn't take my eyes off of him. He moved over to where I was at on the bed and reached out for me.

"Get that shit off." He demanded. "I wanna see my wife naked." He finished with.

I began unzipping my dress with reaching my hands to the back. I guess I was taking too long because Messiah got tired of waiting for me and unzipped it the rest of the way and lifted it fast as hell over my head. Instantly he started sucking on my neck and I knew for a fact that I was gonna have marks left behind. I didn't care though. My body was his to do whatever the fuck he wanted to do with it.

He made his way down between my breasts and squeezed them hard with both his hands. Then used his tongue to circle my nipples, before latching on to one then the other. I caressed his dick with my hand while he was paying attention to my breasts.

He laid me back and then slid his big ass dick in me fast and hard.

"I'm 'bout to make love to you as my wife, ma. Then we're gonna fuck. This shit is real La. It's you and me to the end of time now."

"I love you Messiah. Now make me feel good." I said while moaning from the slow strokes he was giving me.

I didn't have to say that shit again. He really started digging in my damn stomach after that. It was like our bodies were really one and we both completely let go of our thinking and let the feelings take over.

Even though Messiah was talking about making love, the more he kept going the more like straight up fucking we were doing. Its like neither one of us could get enough or go hard enough to satisfy the need we had.

Messiah lifted both my legs over his shoulders. My body was bent up like a fucking pretzel and he had my ass locked where I couldn't do nothing but take the big ass monster dick. He began pounding my pussy and I screamed out back to back from the intense orgasm I was having.

"You not done yet. Turn that ass around." He told my ass while pulling out of me.

I did like he said and tooted my fat ass up while I was arched on all fours. He grazed his hand over my back down between my ass crack and stuck his fingers in my pussy. I held my position and moved back slightly into his hand from his touch.

He slapped me on the ass making that shit jiggle from the impact. Then cupped my cheeks with both hands and leaned in putting his mouth on my pussy from behind. I felt his breath on my ass crack and his tongue going to work. I bucked back against him and started twerking on his face.

Messiah moved his face and tongue away and I missed the feeling. He was really playing right now and knew that I wanted his dick inside me. Shit, my pussy was basically throbbing from how good he was fucking me. He used his fingers again and stuck them in me then pulled them out after fucking me with them for a minute. He replaced his hand with his dick and my breath was instantly taken from me for a second. I felt every inch whenever he was hitting it from the back.

I stayed perfectly still for a minute and so did Messiah while my pussy remained clamped down on his shit. He gripped my ass with one hand and played in my ass with his other hand inserting one finger. That shit made me cum right away and I soaked the bed underneath us.

My wetness gave him the opportunity to begin working his dick in and out of me faster. He plunged in me deeper and deeper until I was face down screaming into the pillow and couldn't move a damn muscle. The shit was hurting so bad and feeling good at the same time. He reached underneath me and rubbed on my clit causing me to cum again. My body was shaking and I couldn't do nothing. His dick really had me fucked up.

"Messiah I can't move, Oh MY GOD!" I screamed out.

"Take the dick. Throw that married pussy on it." He coached me.

I did exactly what the fuck my husband wanted and found enough energy to move. I began throwing it back on him tightening my pussy muscles with each movement he made. That had his ass going wild this time. He grabbed my hips and dug in my guts further than I thought possible.

"Fuck." Was all I could get out.

Messiah always liked to finish on top more than any other position so he could see my pussy and read my expression. So he flipped me around while I felt his body tensing up. I knew his body so well that I could tell when his ass was about to bust. We were so in tune with each other.

He had my knees pressed up against his chest and was letting only the tip of his dick enter in and out of me while he played with my clit with his fingers. That caused me to squirt and as soon as all my cum was out, he moved my legs so that they were wrapped around his waist and he went balls deep.

I pulled him into me through the intense pain and cummed with him again. Our bodies shook and we laid there for a minute catching our breaths before either of us spoke or moved.

We were finally married and I was at peace with everything. This was the best sex we ever had because it was on a whole other level. People who said that married sex was different weren't lying. We really had just become one and I loved him with everything in me.

Even though I knew our night of making love and fucking was just getting started according to Messiah, this shit wouldn't get any better for me. I loved Messiah Lawson and now I was lucky enough to share his last name and hopefully would share many years to come together.

Shanice

The shit I witnessed today was so beautiful to me. My best friend was getting everything she deserved and I was so happy to be able to be a part of her big day. Honestly the day turned out perfect. I was sure that whenever she or Money looked back on today they would be perfectly content with the shit.

The only thing that was off with everything was me and Silk at this point. After talking about it a little this morning on our way here with Larissa I figured she was right and that he knew about me meeting up with my ex last night. I was dumb as hell for trying to do some shit behind Silk's back. Our men were the real fucking deal and I was being reckless.

The truth was I wasn't up to no sneaky shit, but it looked that way in Silk's eyes. I was able to see that. I was also a hypocrite for expecting him to be a hundred percent truthful with me about shit and I was out here being secretive and not telling him about Dre reaching out to me in the first place.

There was just one thing that we both struggled with and that was being honest with shit that we thought would cause hurt or anger the other. We tried to protect each other's feelings so much that we put that above honesty.

For us to make it we were gonna have to stop doing that shit. I believed that after the first time where Silk kept the fact he found out about having a daughter from me he would be honest in the future. Me staying away and really breaking things off for a while showed him that I wouldn't tolerate secrets.

That made what I was up to that much worse. I didn't want Silk to be done with me or for us to have any distance because of the shit I pulled. I got the message already. I wasn't gonna keep a damn thing from him again and was already ready to fix shit now. Seeing him all day, how sexy he was and how perfect his ass was but not being able to talk to him or be near with him was torture enough for me. I wasn't cut out for this being at odds with him at all.

I was determined to fix shit sooner than later and not have us go to sleep tonight without making it right. One thing in my favor was that Silk loved me and was a grown ass man with his shit. He never was for games or holding back his feelings. So I hoped that he was still gonna have that same kind of demeanor when I approached him.

After being sure to keep his distance from me, the two other couples got cozied up leaving the two of us in an awkward position.

This was exactly what I was waiting for. It was now or never.

I took the risk and put myself out there. I stood up from the table and went to where Silk was sitting. Without saying anything I took ahold of his hand that was resting in his lap near his perfect dick. I couldn't stop myself from thinking about that either. I swallowed hard and then pulled his hand.

He knew that I wanted him to come with me. He looked up at me and for the first time, I didn't get the same warm loving look he usually graced me with. Instead his expression was unreadable. It probably didn't help that he had been drinking and smoking more than usual today. I watched him like a hawk and saw how many drinks he threw back tonight alone.

After a moment of the stare off, he took a deep breathe, more like a damn sigh and finally decided to stand up. I was automatically rethinking whether I should even try to have this conversation with him.

Silk was a slow to anger type of nigga. But when he was mad there was no turning back. The fact that he took time to actually think about shit before getting upset made it that much worse when he did. There was another side to Silk that I had never witnessed. But the way he was acting was indicator enough of that shit.

I didn't falter though, I kept a hold of his hand and led him up the steps to the top deck. When we were finally alone I released his hand and turned around so that I was standing face to face with the man I loved.

"I'm sorry." I said the only words worth saying at this point.

I stood there waiting for his reaction, but he didn't say shit back. He stood there looking down at me with the same blank stare and then put his hands in his pockets showing me he was still pissed the fuck off.

"I mean there's nothing going on between me and my ex. I only met up with him to get him to leave me alone. You ain't gotta worry about it no more." I said after taking a deep breath in one rushed statement.

"That's it? You're sorry. My bitch out here meeting with niggas behind my back and I'm supposed to just take that shit. Na, ma that ain't me. That might be that fuckboy you ran back to but I'm not a sucker." He said in a calm voice.

Him talking to me with no feelings in his voice what-so-ever caused a tear to roll down my face. I couldn't even help that shit. Silk never talked to me in a disrespectful way. He wasn't done yet though.

"You know who the fuck I am. I sat outside the whole fuckin' time knowing you was inside your damn parents' house of all places doing some snake ass shit. You been my queen and you straight up play yourself like this, why?" He finished.

"I was trying to keep my ex from fucking up what we got going on. The truth is, I don't know, damn. I just wanted to close that chapter for good I guess." I tried to explain.

"But you couldn't keep shit a hundred with me, the nigga you suppose to love. Shit is fucked up. That nigga coulda tried some real foul shit. You put yourself at risk. And the fucked up part is you shouldn't have wanted to even talk to that bitch ass nigga. On top of the fact that you didn't let me handle him for you." He said.

"I'm sorry. I get it! But I love YOU! Not him. I really get it. I won't keep shit from you. You just gotta give me the chance to prove it."

He was starting to warm up to me. I saw it on his face.

He didn't respond for a good five minutes. He turned around and started pacing and shit. I knew my man was thinking over the shit I told him. I just hoped that he decided to give me another chance. I didn't think I could go with us being apart again.

"Yeah okay. But that nigga dead." He finally said.

I didn't care at this point what happened to Deandre, my hands would be clean when it came to the shit and so would my conscience.

My baby was saying he was gonna give me that chance and we could get past this. I figured he was still skeptical so I was gonna ease his mind. I wasn't gonna keep shit from him from here on out.

I leaned in and wrapped my arms tightly around him inhaling his Tom Ford cologne that I loved so much. I missed the way his body felt next to mine in the short time, less than a day that I wasn't up under him. He put his hands right on my ass and left them there while he put his chin on top of my head. We stood there for a minute before starting to kiss. Shit we were in a full make out session out here.

We did some public shit but for the most part we were private with the fucking we did. So that shit was just gonna have to wait until we got back to the hotel. Now my girl and Money they were some downright freaks out in public with the shit. There was so many times that they were caught fucking and neither one of them really gave a fuck. It was funny as hell, but I guess when Money wanted some pussy nothing stopped him. He got off on people knowing he was liable to fuck anywhere.

I laughed to myself and Silk led me over to the railing where we stood cuddled up looking out at the beautiful port city of Belize City. This was truly a tropical fucking paradise. Times like this, me being held by Silk, were perfect. Shit didn't get better for me.

Messiah

Yesterday's shit was some unspeakable perfection. My family was complete. Now I needed to focus on the business at hand. It was time to lay some mothafuckas out and take over. This plan was over a year in the making and that shit alone had me hyped the fuck up.

It was like after today, I could finally sit back and relax. As long as Emeri was alive I was gonna continue to be looking over my shoulder. I was prepared for the aftermath that came with this damn move and after this shit went down it was gonna be what it was gonna be.

Whether we came out of it alive or not would determine our family's future. I woke up early as hell and had already taken a shower. Now I was getting dressed and LaLa was still asleep in the bed of our hotel suite. I didn't want her to know what was up until after she was out of harm's way. She thought we were staying down here for our honeymoon. But her and the other women were catching a flight in an hour on the same private jet we flew in on. They were heading back to Miami where we would finish out our honeymoon.

The way I set shit up with having everybody except me, Silk, and Draco knowing what was really up was for their protection.

Otherwise I would have told Larissa everything. She was solid when it came to every aspect of my life now and I had a lot of faith in her capabilities. But what we were doing today was trying to take over a cartel. That was some shit I had never even been through before. There was no fucking way my family was gonna be close to this shit.

I didn't want anyone acting strange tipping off Emeri or making him think some shit was up. That was another reason it was on the hush with everybody.

I stood over my wife and my heart swelled with pride. MJ was asleep right next to his mama like he usually was after he somehow found his way in our bed in the middle of the nights where he woke up from a bad dream or some shit. He would crawl right up between us and cozy himself up to his mother. That shit was cool with me, because my lil nigga was my world too. I would go to war with God behind these two.

I leaned down and began kissing on Larissa. How I always did when I woke her up. I began tongue kissing the fuck out of her. She woke up not even a minute after I started and began smiling through the kisses and tried pushing me back. She knew MJ was in bed and wasn't going for my antics just like I knew she wouldn't. I really just wanted to wake her up and get as much action as I could. Shit I didn't know when or if I was coming back.

Soon after MJ was up right next to her. They both smiled up at me.

"Where we going?" Larissa asked with a yawn.

"I gotta go handle some business. You, the kids and the rest of the women are heading back to Miami. We gonna finish our honeymoon back there." I said getting straight to the point and waiting for her response.

I didn't leave any room for argument and she knew that when I said some shit I meant it. I always got my way.

"mhhhhmmmm." She responded with a little attitude and some question in the tone of it.

She stayed where she was in bed, not moving at all and continued to look at me intently. I guess to see what I was gonna say next.

"The Plane leave in an hour. Me and the boys gonna catch up with ya'll tonight."

Finally she got up off the bed and came the few steps over to where I was now sitting putting my Timbs on. Although it was hot as fuck here I needed to dress for battle today so that was how I was suiting up. LaLa probably knew there was more to the shit than what I was telling her.

She reached down and wrapped her arms around me in a tight ass hug. Then pulled back and kissed me deep just like I had been kissing on her to get her to wake up. After that she walked back over to scoop our son up and carried him over to the couch to get him undressed for the bath.

"I love you Mr. Lawson. You better come back to me tonight." She said with a serious undertone.

I was pretty sure that the mention of coming back was because she knew I was gonna do some dangerous shit. She might not know what and I appreciated her not worrying me about the shit. I needed to keep a clear head. There was so many niggas that caught a bullet because they weren't thinking straight at the time.

"You got that ma. I love you too, Mrs. Lawson." I said back to her.

I was the furthest thing from a sappy ass nigga. But my wife and my son were my fuckin' heart. I would never apologize for that shit either. This was the side only a few mothafuckas got to see. Out here in the streets I was heartless and now it was time for me to put all my feelings to the side and let my other side come through.

Me and my day 1's sat outside the property to my father's estate. We were beyond the security cameras and lookout, just up the road parked off in the cut. The spot was beyond the rarely driven road that led to the place.

Draco was smoking like he typically did before some shit like this. Me and Silk usually didn't smoke before to keep our heads about us, but that shit kept Draco focused. He was the type of nigga to have ADHD if his ass didn't smoke some.

None of us were saying shit. There was no point, we already went over the plans so many times there wasn't a question about whether we knew what the fuck to do. We were built for this shit and ready to take what the fuck we came here for.

We were waiting on the phone call to come through from inside the house. I didn't want them to send a message. I needed to hear the nigga's voice on the other line and read from how he sounded if this shit was a set up. My burner cell finally rang with a call. When I answered everything checked out and I was told that shit was a go.

Silk began driving onto the main road and in another couple minutes we pulled up right in front of the big ass gate. There wasn't a security building like I had. Instead there was a tower that sat about a hundred yards within the entrance. Emeri kept two guards on watch at all times rotating shifts.

I learned a lot of shit about keeping my family safe while I was down here. But I also learned from being back home, that even with the best security you could still be touched. My father had become too comfortable down here in Belize.

He hadn't had to face an adversary in over a decade. My wedding was enough to put him at even more ease with the impromptu meeting I asked for yesterday before the ceremony. I didn't really ask in the first place. I basically told his ass I would be stopping by to discuss some important shit. I didn't tell the mothafucka what time but I'm sure his ass knew we were here as soon as we pulled up in front of the gate.

We were let in and drove through the gate after it opened to let us in. Once Silk stopped the car and put it in park all three of us stepped out of the vehicle calm and collected like we planned. I adjusted my clothes and then led the way up to the main front door. There were at least twenty steps made of white alabaster stone that led up to the door. My father was an over the top nigga. He went all out when it came to the shit he owned.

I knocked a few times and the security guards at the door opened it wide. As soon as we stepped inside they began the usual process of checking each of us for weapons.

The difference this time was that security had already flipped. All except for my father's most loyal right hand that was by his sides nine times out of ten.

That was the nigga Silk and Draco already planned to divert. There was a small bomb placed where we had been parked off the road before driving up. All Silk needed to do was place a call once I was inside the office with my father and then draw away his partna.

That way I would be face to face with him and able to take him out without a problem. I was gonna make the shit quick with a bullet to the head. There was no time for any of that sentimental shit.

The security pretended not to notice our heat when they fake patted us down. I had my pistol and nine on me. I already knew that my niggas were strapped and ready to bust too. Silk and Draco were led out to the patio off the main foyer and I was led to Emeri's office. Shit was moving according plan perfect.

I stood inside the big ass office with my hands ready to draw my shit as soon as needed. My father sat behind the desk that was positioned in front of the big ass window overlooking the gardens. He looked right at me with a smirk on his face, like he thought some shit was funny. I got a bad feeling about our plan. As soon as the doubt clouded my mind his right hand had a gun pointed at me.

I kept my hand on my hip where one of my guns was. At this point it was clear that he knew some shit was up. I didn't know if all the security was in on him knowing about the shit or just these two niggas in the room.

Emeri started clapping his hands slow and dramatic, loud as hell.

"I applaud your effort boy, but I am your father after all. You should have known better than think you could go against me." He said.

Before I was able to respond there was a loud ass sound that must have been the explosion Silk or Draco set off. I didn't know who was out there with them at this point. But I was confident that they could handle themselves and hopefully we would all make it out this shit alive.

I didn't give a fuck about the nigga aiming the gun at me. I wasn't a bitch and had been held at gunpoint before so this wasn't new to me. I still wasn't gonna say shit. It was clear that Emeri thought he had every fucking thing figured out.

"The fuck you mean pops?" I asked trying to play the whole thing off.

His best friend and personal body guard Saul walked over to where I was standing. He threw a punch and landed that shit right on the side of my eye. I still kept my hand on my heat and took the mothafuckin' punch without letting that shit knock me off balance much. I stared the nigga down the whole fucking time too.

He was lucky right now that it was two against one. Shit that wasn't even the fucking reason I wasn't swinging back on his ass. It was only because if I was caught up in a damn brawl with this nigga then I wouldn't be able to keep an eye on Emeri. There was no way I was letting his ass out of my damn sight.

Even though shit was going left I still was determined to body both these mothafuckas and come out on top of everything. I was either leaving dead or alive and in charge of the cartel.

"You sealed your fate coming against me, but I need to know how many of my men you turned as well." My father said while standing to his feet.

"Fuck you. I ain't saying shit." I said looking back at him with murder in my eyes.

This was the first time he ever got the real attitude and look from me that I actually felt. I never let my true emotions show when it came to business. But when it came to murder the gangsta came out.

"Oh I see now... You got daddy issues and letting that control your moves." He said before tisking and continuing, "Now look where that got you." The more he talked the deeper his accent got showing that he was more upset about the shit then he was letting on.

He finally pulled his weapon out and I wasn't surprised that he was holding his pocket knife. The shit was what he always carried. He told me that killing a person up close was how he was able to sleep at night. Knowing that they were dead and being able to look the nigga in the eyes as the life drained out of them was important to him. He was a heartless nigga but shit I wasn't too much different. I guess some things were inherited.

He came over to where I was and stood only a few inches away. He held the knife to my neck and dug that shit in where he held it firm. We stood there, both of us not moving.

There were some more noises coming from outside the door towards the front of the house where we entered in. A few shots rang out and then I heard footsteps running out of the house.

Still we were almost fucking paralyzed standing still. I wasn't even paying attention to where the fuck his nigga was at anymore. It was just me and the man who gave me life. That was all he was to me anyway. Fuck what he thought.

All of the sudden the door to Emeri's office swung open and in walked the same nigga who continued to get in my damn way. I turned my head to the side to see exactly what the fuck he was up to. Fuck the knife being held to my neck. If Emeri was gonna slice my throat he was gonna do that shit. My hands were still free and one of them rested comfortably on my piece.

Shit was just getting more and more interesting and I needed to let it play out. Emeri didn't look surprised to see Antoine and that had me thinking he was somehow part of the reason Emeri knew I was up to some shit. It would be just like his stupid ass to get in my fucking way again. That was how he rolled.

With Antoine coming through the door, Emeri lowered the knife from my neck but kept it close. Antoine got closer to where we were at and that's when I noticed he wasn't alone. My older brother Biz and Draco busted in fast as hell right behind him. Bizz instantly let off two in my father's right hand Saul.

Before I even grabbed my shit, Antoine aimed his shit at Emeri and pulled the trigger. I didn't know what the fuck was going on or why Antoine was here trying to save me or take out our father.

Emeri fell to the ground and I stood there wondering what the fuck my brother was doing here with this nigga. I turned around to gauge what the fuck was going on in the room. Biz and Antoine were standing near each other while Draco was beside me.

"The fuck is going on bruh?" I asked looking at my damn brother. My real brother that was.

"Antoine came through and got up with me as soon as he got wind of the shit Emeri was up to. Apparently he knew all about your plan to take over and even had that bitch Che in on some shit to go against you. I came down last night and met up with Toine. We had to take care of the guards who stayed loyal to his ass first, then we hurried the fuck up here to get your ass." He said telling me everything he knew.

The shit he was spitting was fucked up. He was basically saying that the nigga Antoine was the one I should be thanking for making shit possible for the takeover that was about to happen. There was no fuckin' way I would ever be good with that nigga. Shit he was still the same nigga who came against me in my eyes. He moved to my city, fucked my wife and continued to step on my damn toes.

No way was I gonna be calling him by nicknames and shit like my older brother was doing now. Shit we already made an agreement from him coming through with the Fe shit that I wasn't gonna murder his ass. Wasn't nothing left for his ass to get from me.

If he was looking to get a cut from our family business that we just inherited that shit wasn't about to happen. He could work and cop all his shit from our family deals if he wanted but he was still in with the Italians and Larissa's family anyway. I hoped his ass didn't expect shit because I might just have to go back on my promise to LaLa about not killing the nigga.

"Word." was all I said. "Where's Silk?" I asked changing the subject.

"Watch out!" Draco yelled out before slamming into me.

Draco must have saw that Emeri wasn't dead from the shot Antoine took at him. He used his gun and sent a few bullets in Emeri's direction while he pushed me out of the way saving me from the bullet that Emeri sent my way.

Emeri's body slumped to the ground immediately again. Draco hit him with a head shot and I knew for a fact the mothafucka was dead now.

Draco's weight shifted into me again but this time when I looked over at him I realized he had been hit by the bullet intended for me. My nigga had pushed me aside and took a bullet for me.

Draco was hit in the chest and losing a lot of fucking blood. His face was pale as shit and I tried to stand him up and brace all of his weight while I walked him out of the room fast as hell.

226

His entire body collapsed to the floor before we made it two steps. I was yelling for Biz to help me and tried lifting him back up to carry him down to my car. I needed to get him to the hospital right the fuck away. But when I looked down I saw his life bleeding out of him.

His chest was soaked with blood and I tried to cover the wound with my hands and apply some pressure. I knew there wasn't no fucking ambulances coming. My nigga's breathing slowed and he took his last breath in my arms within a minute.

There wasn't a time I ever shed a single fucking tear, but when my cousin who was my damn brother died in my arms my tears flowed. Silk finally came in the office and saw me on the floor next to Draco. He pulled me up and we both carried him out.

We both felt the same pain with the loss of Draco. The shit was still fresh on my mind and I couldn't even come to terms with the shit. I had questioned Draco's loyalty and today he saved my fucking life. He was the reason I was still living and I didn't know how I was gonna make it through this shit.

The ride to the small airport was hard as hell. I called and made arrangements for Draco's body to be transported with us. Everything was too damn unreal. We would keep going and building as a team. But shit would never be the same again. Draco was gone.

Today was all the way fucked up. I would gladly have let that bullet hit me instead of Draco if it meant he would still be alive. My nigga didn't even get a chance to really live. I was the boss, the head of it all but that shit came at a great cost.

I knew this was the shit we chose but it didn't make it an easier pill to swallow.

By the time we made it to Miami it was the middle of the night. Larissa was asleep when I walked into the hotel room. MJ was asleep in bed right beside her. The shit was almost exactly like it was when I left them before heading out in Belize. These two were my peace.

I undressed down to my boxers and pulled back the covers. I already showered and everything before I caught a flight back. The shit that happened today had my head fucked up but being here with my family would hopefully ease the pain I was feeling some.

Larissa turned over and opened her eyes. She must have only been half asleep waiting on me to make it back to her.

"Everything good?" She asked.

"As long as I got your love and loyalty I'm good shorty." I said back before leaning towards her and placing a kiss on her forehead.

This hood love was a fucking rollercoaster. The shit we all went through together was filled with the best and worst shit. Yesterday love conquered with my marriage to Larissa and today Draco's loyalty let me make it back to my damn family.

So when I said that shit to Larissa I meant every fucking word. All I could hope for was a future filled with both love and loyalty and that would be enough for me. But I knew that whatever we went through we would go through that shit together. Larissa Lawson was mine and I was hers.

My wife put her arm around me and we drifted off to sleep.

The End...